"TECHR"

To Ashley —
You are a
great "TECHR" —
John Burroughs

JO ANN BURROUGHS

"TECHR"

Faith Printing
Taylors, South Carolina

First Printing
November, 2003

ISBN 1-931600-64-3

The illustration for the cover of "*TECHR*" was done by **Linda McCaslin** of North Augusta, South Carolina.

*This book is dedicated to my four grandchildren,
who bring so much joy into my life…*

~IOULI~
*My only grandson…the first to steal my heart and give me
bragging rights…*

~ANASTASIA~
*My first granddaughter…a precious beauty who gave me
the name, MamMa…*

~JESSICA~
*My perfect, miracle grandchild who defied all odds to
survive a premature birth…*

~MADALYN~
*My youngest granddaughter…the sweetest New Year's
Eve present I ever received…*

*And***to LITTLE WILL****
*The precious grandson I never got to know…
the Littlest Angel in Heaven…*

AUTHOR'S NOTE

BEFORE I BEGAN this book, I struggled with how to continue the story of *JOHNATHON* and keep true experiences encompassed in the context of the unfolding drama. After witnessing the real-life birth of my last granddaughter, it became very clear to me that the miracle surrounding a child's life is worthy of telling, whether through fact or fiction.

So ..."TECHR" is a work of fiction entwined around a composite of true stories about children. Most of the stories about the children in "TECHR" happened to me when I was a teacher. Some of the accounts happened to other teachers I have known or were experiences I have actually witnessed through my close involvement in schools.

Even though the character of "Johnny" is a figment of my imagination, I'm sure his situation has magnified itself many times over as people struggle with what they should do with their lives.

It is my fervent prayer that, by reading "TECHR," more people will feel compelled to reach out to children who are abused, lonely, and hurting. A hug or a smile doesn't cost us anything…but the payback is incomprehensible when a child's life is snatched from the jaws of failure and lifted to a future that is full of hope and love.

Jo Ann Burroughs

“TECHR”

ONE

IT WAS A GRAY, dismal day as the rain steadily dripped from my hair and mingled with the tears that made rivulets down my face. I stared at the casket when my dad's doctor friends carefully placed it on the gaping hole that had only been dug a few hours before. I felt Dad's shoulders tense when the funeral attendants placed the spray of red roses on the casket. I reached over and grabbed his hand as I had done so many times when I was a little boy. He looked over at me and smiled through his tears. Even in his sorrow, his look comforted me just as the still, cold body in the casket had comforted him so many times in his life.

The minister moved near the casket and read the usual verses of scripture that are heard at funerals. I suppose that the verses were fitting. I didn't really listen carefully. All I could think about was the pressure of Dad's hand and the enormous pain I felt in my heart.

After the final prayer, my mother and my sister, Tara, walked over to the casket and placed single, yellow roses next to the huge spray of red ones. It was so like Tara to remember the yellow roses. I felt a twinge of jealousy as I wished I had remembered the yellow roses. But the jealousy faded quickly when my turn came to make my way to the casket. I pried Dad's fingers loose from mine and stumbled a bit as I walked to the gray, metal coffin that looked so cold and forlorn. I clumsily reached into the inside pocket of my black suit jacket and brought out a crumpled note held together by a paper clip. Through a blur of tears I placed the unsightly note next to the perfect yellow roses and returned quietly to my seat.

As if by magic, what seemed like hundreds of somber and red-eyed children started filing by the casket, placing myriads of objects, flowers, and child-made drawings on the fresh dirt that surrounded the burial place. Not a sound was heard from the children except for the gentle scuffling of hundreds of little worn tennis shoes crunching over the new dirt and the sniffling of runny noses and muffled cries that only children with broken hearts can make.

Dad was next. It seemed like an eternity before he finally stood up and made his way to the casket. Mom, Tara, and I glanced nervously at each other, wondering how Dad would survive this final goodbye and watching to see what would be the last gift he gave to the person who had loved him most in his life. My dad, Dr. Johnathon Adams, the renowned doctor; the world famous heart surgeon; the pioneer in cardiac procedures; always the doctor, slowly reached into his side pocket and pulled out an old stethoscope…not a real one, but a toy; ragged, discolored, and practically worn out from hours of playing and pretending when he was a child. Dad gently caressed the old stethoscope, looked at it lovingly, and carefully placed it on the casket. All in attendance wept openly as this great man knelt down before the casket and said, "Goodbye, Techr….I love you."

TWO

THE RIDE BACK from the little, country church cemetery was quiet. Mom and Tara sat across from Dad and me in the long, black limo, each one of us staring out into space and remembering. Dad had insisted on the limo, even though we were not family. Actually, 'Techr' had no real family, unless you can count the hundreds of kids she had taught over the past sixty-one years. Dad thought of her as his mother, so that pretty much made her my grandmother. I had another grandmother on my Mom's side, but not like 'Techr.' She was just special. My thoughts drifted back to the first time I met this great lady.

It was Christmas Day, twenty years ago. I must have been about four or five years old at the time. After the early morning Christmas ritual at our large home in Atlanta, Dad announced that we were going on a surprise trip to a little rural town in South Carolina. We packed hurriedly, loaded down our car with toys, suitcases, the family dog, Old Bill, and we headed out.

"Where are we going, Daddy?" I asked as we rode down the busy interstate.

Dad looked into the rearview mirror and smiled at me. "I am finally taking you to meet your grandmother."

"But this isn't the way to Nanny's house. Why are we going this way?"

"Oh, you're not going to see Nanny. Besides, you see her all the time. You're going to meet my mother!"

"John, I think you'd better tell them the truth," Mom said in a low voice.

Dad gave Mom a furtive look, reached over and held her hand, and nodded in agreement. Looking back at me in the mirror, he said, "Johnny, the lady we're going to see today is not your real grandmother. She's not my real mother, either. I don't know where my real mother is. I lost track of her a long time ago when she abandoned me at a bus station somewhere in Florida. I don't know where she is, and I don't really care. You see, Johnny, my real mother was not a very nice person."

I remember quizzing Dad about his mother, but he didn't seem to want to talk about her too much. It wasn't until years later that I found out Dad had been severely abused by his mother and dad. Both of his parents had been alcoholics and in and out of prison more times than you can count. Dad had a tumultuous childhood to say the least, and spent a lot of his formative years in foster homes or homes for abused children.

That Christmas morning as we rode along on our surprise visit, I watched my dad's face go from dark and stormy as he talked about his real mom, to bright and cheerful when he reminisced about the "Mother" we were heading to visit.

"Johnny, this 'grandmother' that you are going to meet today was actually my first grade teacher. I loved her the moment I met her. She was the kindest and most caring person who ever came into my life, and you know what, Johnny? She loved me, and she listened to me, and she taught me to believe in myself. I called her 'Techr,' from the first day that I met her, and she didn't seem to mind at all. As a matter of fact, I didn't know her real name for a long time. Her name is Mrs. Ellie Harris, so when you meet her today, you can call her Mrs. Harris."

"I think I will call her 'Techr,' too, if that's all right, Daddy." I saw my dad's face light up like a light bulb when I said that.

"Well, I think 'Techr' will be mighty proud for you to call her that, Son. You know, she doesn't even know that I have children of my own. When I performed her heart surgery a while back, I was so excited to see her and to mend her sick heart that I completely forgot to mention all of you guys. She will be so surprised!"

We rode on in silence for a while, and I could tell my dad was thinking back to this teacher who had meant so much to him. Every now and then he would smile, and sometimes laugh out loud as he recalled days with 'Techr' when he was in her first grade class.

I repeatedly asked Daddy to tell me why he was smiling, and he would rattle off story after story about his year with 'Techr.' By the time we drove up to 'Techr's' house, I felt like I knew this new "grandmother" about as well as he did.

Boy! Was 'Techr' surprised when we walked up to her door! Dad was right. 'Techr' was everything he had said she would be. She took to Tara and me right off, and we had the best Christmas I can ever remember. It was that Christmas that we became 'Techr's' family. Her husband had been dead for a while, and she had no children of her own. So, without anybody saying anything, Dad became 'Techr's' son; Mom was her daughter-in-law; Tara, her beautiful granddaughter; and me? She always said I was the best grandson a person could have!

For the last twenty years, Tara and I have spent holidays and summer vacations with 'Techr.' Dad and Mom came, too, when they could get away from their demanding jobs. I guess I went to stay with her the most. I really don't know why except that we formed a bond right from the start, and I loved that old lady with every fiber of my being. I guess I took over where Dad left off. Of course, my name being "Johnathon" didn't hurt any, either. I think 'Techr' often thought of me as the same little Johnathon whom she had taught and loved so many years back. I have to admit that I sure do look a lot like my dad.

THREE

'TECHR'S' HOUSE FELT cold and lonely when we walked in after the funeral was over. Mom and Tara went to the kitchen and started uncovering and heating the stacks of casseroles that were piled in the ancient refrigerator. I stood in the doorway and looked at the fried chicken boxes on the counter. I smiled as I thought how much 'Techr' would have liked that chicken! Even though Dad had warned her over and over about eating grease, she just could not give up the fried chicken. Dad didn't know it, but every time I went to see 'Techr', I stopped by and bought her a box of the really greasy kind with the thick, crispy skin. What fun we had eating that chicken and crunching every morsel that fell into the box! I guess I somehow contributed to 'Techr's' heart failing in the end, but I couldn't deny her anything, and those times we were "Partners in Crime" eating fried chicken were some of my favorite times with 'Techr.'

We had only been back at 'Techr's' house a few

minutes when scores of people started coming in to pay their respects to us, 'Techr's' family. Some I recognized, especially the teachers from the school where 'Techr' had spent nearly sixty years in the same room.

Dad and I moved about the room and listened to so many stories the teachers were telling about 'Techr.' Some I had heard first-hand; others were new to me. I couldn't help but smile when I heard the principal of the school tell about the summer the school was being renovated , and 'Techr' showed up each day in "HER" room, telling the workmen everything to do. She drove the workers crazy, but "HER" room was fixed up just like she wanted it to be!

As I milled about the small house, I saw people of all ages wandering about. Some were people about Dad's age; others were in their thirties; and then there were the children. I didn't count them, but it must have been several hundred people who wandered in and out through the course of the afternoon. I assumed most of the mourners were students 'Techr' had touched over the years. People from all walks of life. People who all had one thing in common. They all loved 'Techr.'

When the final piece of fried chicken was gone; the last casserole dish cleaned and stacked for returning; and the door closed on the visitor who had lingered the longest, we all sat down around the kitchen table in silence.

"Well, that's it," Dad said quietly. "Our precious 'Techr' is gone, and there'll never be another one like her. I'll call someone tomorrow to come over and clear out her things so we can put the house up for sale."

I panicked! "No, Dad! You can't just have anyone come into 'Techr's' house and mess with her stuff! We have to do it, Dad! We can stay a few days and make sure everything is done right! You know 'Techr' would want us to do it."

"Son, I have to be back in Atlanta by day after tomorrow. I have two surgeries scheduled that cannot wait another day. Mom will have mamas and babies lined up in the waiting room of the Children's Clinic anticipating her return. Your sister has only been working with Dr. Lanford a few weeks, and he doesn't have another RN who is trained to assist him in surgery. And you, Son! You're in your second year of medical school. Do you think you can afford to miss any more days and still keep up with your work?"

"I can't see that another day or two will hurt any. You know yourself, Dad, that I don't have to attend classes that much as long as I get the lecture notes from someone. I don't have any quizzes coming up for another three weeks. We owe 'Techr' this, Dad. Look what she did for you, Dad! For all of us! She was always there for us; now we have to be here for her!"

Dad shook his head. I looked at Mom who had tears slowly trickling down her face. "Please, Mom, talk to Dad. We have to do this for 'Techr'."

"I'm sorry, Johnny. Dad's right. We have to go and get on with our busy lives. That's what 'Techr' would want us to do. We're all in the business of saving lives, Johnny, and people are depending on us to be there for them. We all have to go, Johnny. Our flights leave early in the morning, and we must be on them."

"I'm not going, Mom. You and Dad and Tara go ahead, but I'm not going. Not yet. I have to stay here long enough to get 'Techr's' affairs in order. I have to make sure all of her things that she has accumulated over the last eighty-one years are not just thrown to the wind or stuffed in black plastic bags to be dumped with the garbage. I have to do this, Mom. Dad, I have to do this for 'Techr'."

Dad looked sadly at me with those piercing brown eyes that were so like mine. "What about med school, Johnny? You can't just throw away all you have worked for to rummage through thousands of children's notes and pictures that 'Techr' probably has stashed in every nook and cranny of this old house! I loved her, too, Johnny! Lord, how I loved her! But I have to leave behind this wonderful old house and all the stuff that she had. I will take one thing with me tomorrow, Johnny. That's the confidence that she gave me to become somebody important. Oh, and the memories! I'll carry those memories of 'Techr' with me as long as I live!"

I looked straight into Dad's tear-filled eyes. "You go, Dad. I know you have to go. You, too, Mom, Tara. Go! I understand why you need to leave on that flight tomorrow. But I also hope that you understand why I cannot go with you. This is something I have to do. I promise, I'll only stay as long as it takes to sort through 'Techr's' things. Then I'll go back to school."

Mom looked at me with understanding that only moms

can have. She laid her hand on Dad's arm and squeezed it gently. He looked at her face, and then turned back to me.

"Okay, Son. Stay if you must. But I'm counting on you to get back to school in a day, no less than two. You cannot miss too much, Johnny. You are destined to be a doctor, a great doctor! We've planned this for you. You have the ability and the compassion to be the best doctor this country has ever seen. Don't throw it away, Johnny. Think about what you're doing!"

"I will, Dad. I think about it all the time. I know you are counting on me to follow in your footsteps. I've known that all my life."

"Remember, Johnny, a day – no more than two."

FOUR

A DAY, NO MORE THAN TWO, quickly turned into a week, then two. I knew I should leave and go back to school as I had promised Dad that I would. But I couldn't. Every time I went through a box of 'Techr's' collected treasures, I found myself mesmerized and felt I had to look at each note, picture, and card that she had found too precious to discard.

Most of the boxes contained children's drawings and carefully scrawled notes that only a first grader could create. I read over and over, "I luv you, Techr," signed Billy, Joe, Todd, Kathy, Miguel, Shannon, George, Mary, Patrick, Amy, Roy, Ann, Marty, Steve, Sveta, Joni, Lisa, Sherry, Roosevelt, Ruth, Jessica, Chris…the list went on and on. At the bottom of one of the boxes I even found a note signed, "Johnathon." That had to be my dad. 'Techr' always said she only taught one Johnathon, my dad.

I stared at the childish note written so long ago by my dad when the shrill ringing of the phone broke my concentration. I said a silent prayer that it would not be Dad again demanding that I get back to med school.

My prayer was answered when the voice on the other end of the line was female, one that sounded vaguely familiar. "Is this Ellie Harris' residence?"

"Yes, it is," I replied. "Can I help you?"

With a bit of hesitation the person continued. "This is Shelli Foster, principal at Andrews Elementary School. I'm looking for Johnathon Adams. I understand he is staying in Miss Ellie's home for a while."

"It's me, Mrs. Foster. I'm Johnathon – uh, not the doctor; I'm the doctor's son."

"Hi, Johnathon. Yes, I know you're the younger Johnathon Adams. I've seen you several times at the school in Miss Ellie's room when you were visiting her. I understand from some of Miss Ellie's neighbors that you have been staying in her house to sort through her things."

"Yes, Ma'am. I had only planned to stay a day or two but I can't seem to finish the task, and I'm not leaving until I do."

"Well, Johnathon, you are called Johnathon, aren't you?"

"Actually, Mrs. Foster, my family and friends call me, Johnny, but I answer to most anything."

"Well, Johnny sounds good to me. Johnny, I need a great big favor. You know that I have not been able to fill Miss Ellie's position since she passed away during the school year. I'm looking every day for a replacement for her to fill out the school year, but so far, I've had no luck finding anyone willing to take her first grade class. Unfortunately, because it is flu season, all of the usual substitutes are taken, and I've had to split up her class among the other first grade teachers since Ellie's death. I really need someone with a four year degree to take over her class. Johnny, are you planning on going back to school this term? I thought if you're not, then you might be interested in helping me with Ellie's class until I can find a suitable replacement."

"Mrs. Foster! Me! I'm not a teacher! I'm a medical student. I'm supposed to be in school right now, but I just can't leave yet. I'm having a friend of mine fax lecture notes to me here at 'Techr's' house, so I'm kind of keeping up. I really need to put in some study time soon because I have some quizzes coming up in a few days. My dad will probably kill me if I mess this semester up. I should have gone from here over two weeks ago, but I just can't make myself leave. I will have to go back soon and face my professors and my dad. I don't know which I'm dreading the most. Probably my dad! So you see, Mrs. Foster, I can't help you out with 'Techr's' students because I won't be here much longer. And besides, like I said, I'm not a teacher!"

"Well, Johnny, from all the stories I heard from Ellie about you, I thought maybe you'd follow in her footsteps. But a doctor? Wow! Ellie didn't tell me that you were going to be a doctor, too! That's great! But if for some reason you decide to stay longer, instead of going back to school this term, just give some thought to my proposal.

I'm at school every day until after 5pm, so if you change your mind, you can call me there. I surely would like to hear from you!"

"Oh, you won't hear from me, Mrs. Foster. I'm really sorry I can't help you, and I certainly do appreciate the offer, but, like I said, I'm not a teacher!"

FIVE

AT EIGHT O'CLOCK the next morning, I was standing in Mrs. Foster's office. A surprised look came over the principal's face when she looked up and saw me standing there. "Johnny? I sure didn't expect to see you today."

I looked down at my feet and shifted uncomfortably. "Uh, Mrs. Foster, I didn't expect to be here either. But after I talked to you last night, I thought a lot about what you said. I couldn't even sleep for thinking how 'Techr's' students need somebody to take over for her until a really good teacher can be found. Well, I thought, uh, that I might be able to give it a try for a day or two since I'm here in town and all. That is, if you still want me to."

"Oh, yes, Johnny, I still need you. Can you start today? Those poor kids are scattered from room to room! They will be so excited to get back to familiar surroundings."

"Today? Uh, well, I guess I can. Now I don't know what to do. Will somebody help me?"

"Sure we will. Actually, Ellie left lesson plans for a

month, so there should be plans for at least two weeks left. Come on, let me take you to her room and go over the schedule for the day. Oh, you already know where her room is, don't you, Johnny? You've been over here so many times."

"Yes, Ma'am, I do. But it sure will seem strange without 'Techr' in it."

I followed the principal down the hall to 'Techr's' room. The door was locked, and the room was dark and quiet. Mrs. Foster fumbled through at least fifty keys on a big, metal ring before she found the right one. I walked in the room I had frequented so many times in the past. The desks were all in straight rows, just like 'Techr' had left them that last day she had been there. I looked at her familiar handwriting on the boards; the early morning math that she had so carefully written with a red pen, and I couldn't help but smile. She had hated those boards with a passion. She was from the "old school" and thought that only chalkboards should be used in classrooms.

The principal walked over to 'Techr's' desk and rumbled through some stacks until she found the lesson plan book. She handed it to me. "I'd bet my last dollar that those plans are about perfect, Johnny. Why don't you study them for a while, look over the teachers' editions, and get prepared for the children to come back into the room right after lunch. How does that sound to you?"

My eyes rolled back in my head. "It sounds pretty doggone scary to me, if you want to know the truth, Mrs.

Foster. What if I can't get prepared by lunch? Could I wait and get the children tomorrow?"

Mrs. Foster smiled. "You'll be ready, Johnny. They're just first graders. I'll bring them to you right after they eat lunch, okay?"

I closed my eyes and sighed. "Okay. I'll try to be ready, Mrs. Foster." The principal left the room, and I sank down in 'Techr's' old comfortable, black chair. My knees were trembling, my palms were sweating, and my heart rate was about double its usual speed. To tell the truth, I was scared silly of those twenty-one, "just first graders!"

SIX

THE MORNING FLEW by extremely fast as I searched through the books and materials that 'Techr' had used with such ease. I almost panicked when I looked up at the big, black clock on the wall and saw that it was nearly eleven o'clock! I wasn't ready!

I had just about talked myself into leaving the room and the school and never looking back, when I heard the door open. I looked slowly around and watched in awe as twenty-one first graders filed quietly into the room and took their places in the rows of desks. My mouth dropped open slightly, and my eyes darted from child to child. Forty-two eyes were staring back at me. I quickly looked back at the door as it closed, and it was at that moment I realized that I was completely alone with all those little people. I knew I needed to say something, but all I could do was look at them! It was like a stare down; them looking at me and me looking at them.

Finally, the silence was broken by a small voice in the

back of the room. "Are you our Techr?"

I eased my head around to see who had spoken. I couldn't tell from my angle behind 'Techr's' desk. Reluctantly, I rose from the chair and walked to the center of the room. "Well, I guess I am your teacher for a while, but not for long. I'm just filling in until Mrs. Foster can find you a real teacher." My voice quivered like it had never done before, and beads of sweat popped out on my forehead.

"You ain't no real techr? What'cha doing here then?" It was the same kid from the back of the room. I eased my head over and spotted the small culprit who was asking questions. It was a tiny, little boy with red, curly hair and a face full of freckles. His small feet dangled from his chair, and he had his head resting on one hand, while the index finger on the other hand was busy digging in his nose.

I rolled my eyes upward, asking for divine guidance on what to do. Since I got no immediate answers from that direction, I figured I was on my own. "No, I am not a real teacher, uh, what is your name?"

The little guy with the freckles quit digging long enough to answer, "Percival."

"Percival? Your name is Percival? Oh, Lawdy!" I couldn't believe that this tiny child already tagged with kinky, red hair and freckles and a finger totally out of control could possibly be humiliated further by having the name, Percival!

I leaned over to look at this "Percival" again, expecting another question at any moment. But Percival had put his face in the crook of his arm and wouldn't look at me. I walked slowly back to his desk and knelt down next to him.

"Percival? You under there?"

A pair of big, blue eyes peeked out at me. "Hey, Buddy, I think Percival is, uh, some kind of name. It's different and uh, kind of catchy, and, uh, I bet you don't have any friends with that name." I about panicked when the big, blue eyes watered up with tears. I decided to leave the Percival problem for a while and walked back to the front of the room. As I looked up, I found every face in the classroom looking at me as if I had committed the crime of the century.

"What? Why are you looking at me that way? I didn't mean to make Percival feel bad about his name. I just didn't know anyone was ever named Percival, that's all."

A chorus of "ooh-ooh" sounded, in unison, from the twenty little people who were staring at me. A mournful wail came from the back row where Percival was sobbing loudly now. Sweat popped out on my forehead and trickled down my face. I looked at the clock. It was only 11:30 in the morning. I had three more hours to go before it would be time to send Percival and his twenty cheerleaders home for the day! Those were the longest three hours of my life!

SEVEN

AFTER TOSSING AND turning in my old bed at 'Techr's' house, I finally got up at 3AM and turned on the lights. I looked around the room that I had claimed for so many years. The walls were adorned with my childish drawings, framed neatly with hand cut borders that I had helped 'Techr' make.

One of the pictures was bigger than the others. It was a picture I had drawn of me giving 'Techr' a bunch of yellow flowers. I thought back to the time I had given 'Techr' that picture. It was on her birthday, and I had forgotten about it. My sister, Tara, hadn't forgotten it though. She was like that. I remember at supper that night, Tara smugly asked me if I had sent 'Techr' something for her birthday. My heart sank. I had forgotten.

"Well, I sent her a card with beautiful red roses all over it 'cause 'Techr' loves roses. And, I also included one of my school pictures in it. The last time we were visiting her, she said that she wanted some pictures of us." Tara smiled that thirteen year old smile at me, and if Dad and Mom had not been watching, I probably would have smacked her right on that smug smile of hers.

I ran to my room and got out some paper and crayons. In my nine year old mind, I had to do something for 'Techr' that was better than Tara's card and picture. So I drew a picture that was supposed to be 'Techr' and me. Since Tara had said that 'Techr' loved flowers, I drew myself handing 'Techr' a bundle of flowers – big, yellow flowers that I meant to be roses, although they looked more like wop-sided sunflowers. I had to make them yellow because I had lost my red crayon. I wrote in a purple crayon at the bottom of the picture; *Birthday flowers from Johnny – I hope you like 'em.*

'Techr' wrote both of us back and thanked us for the special gifts we had sent. She didn't say a thing about my picture arriving late. She told Tara that she loved her school picture and had put it on her desk at school so she could look at her favorite girl each day. She told me that my drawing was just perfect and asked me how I knew that yellow roses were her favorite. I felt ten feet tall that day when I read my note. I think I might have even bragged to Tara that 'Techr's' favorite flowers were yellow roses.

'Techr' always knew how to handle children. She had a knack for doing and saying just the right things that made children feel good about themselves.

So, what was wrong with me? I had just spent three hours with twenty-one children and had managed to humiliate one because of his name, and the other twenty already hated me because I had hurt their classmate and friend.

Maybe I shouldn't go back. But I had promised Mrs. Foster that I would stick it out until she could find a certified teacher who was trained in dealing with six year olds. But what was I to do in the meantime?

"Oh, 'Techr!' I need your advice so badly right now." I looked Heavenward and sighed deeply. "Okay, I guess I'm on my own, eh? I can do this. If you were able to handle these little people for sixty years, I know I can handle them for a few days. I'll do better tomorrow. You just wait and see. Yeah, I'll do a whole lot better tomorrow. You'll be proud of me tomorrow, 'Techr'."

I turned out the light and stared at the dark until the clock on the nightstand disturbed my sleepless state. It was time to get ready for school again. I felt a little nauseous, but knew I couldn't stay home. After all, I was the teacher!

EIGHT

THE LATE BELL was ringing when I arrived at the school. *Well, Buddy*, I thought to myself. *My second day as a teacher, and I'm late.*

I hurried from the teachers' parking lot and entered the school by the side door, hoping to avoid the principal. But, no. There she came around the corner, cheerfully talking to some kids who were walking to their classrooms. "Hi, Mr. Adams. I'm glad to see you back this morning." Mrs. Foster glanced at her watch, then looked back at me and smiled. "I'm sure your students are waiting anxiously for you. Have a great day!"

I rolled my eyes back in my head as I was so prone to do when frustrations got the better of me. Slowly walking down the long hall, I noticed teachers in all of the classrooms, except mine. I took a deep breath and entered "my" room.

The twenty-one first graders were all in their seats, staring at the door as I entered. "Aw, shucks! You back agin? I thought we wuz goin' to have a substute!" It was none other than Percival, all revived and ready to attack me again.

"Good morning, boys and girls," I managed to reply to Percival's somewhat less than enthusiastic greeting. "Yes, I'm back. I, uh, I'm sorry I'm a little bit late, but I made it as fast as I could."

"That's 'cause you ain't no real techr. A real techr comes early and stands at the door when we come in so we won't hit nobody or nuttin'." Percival again!

Biting my tongue to keep from saying something that would set Percival off again, I replied, "Well, Percival, I'll try to be here real early tomorrow, and I'll bet that I even beat you here. How about that?"

"You'll shore 'nuff beat me tomorrow, Techr, 'cause I ain't comin' tomorrow." Percival looked around at the other kids, and they all begin to snicker.

"What's so funny? Why are you laughing? I don't think it's a bit funny that Percival is not coming to school tomorrow!" I put my hands on my hips for effect, the same way I'd seen 'Techr' do so many times.

"Ain't none of us coming tomorrow, Techr," a little brown-eyed boy in the front row replied. "Tomorrow's Saturdy, and nobody comes on Saturdy."

I felt the red creep slowly up my face. It was 8:15 AM, my second day as a teacher. The day went downhill from there!

NINE

ABOUT TEN O'CLOCK that same morning, after I had struggled through a story in reading about some robot that liked to eat pizza, the lady from the lunchroom appeared at the door. "Excuse me, but I didn't get your lunch form this morning," the lunchroom lady said, solemnly.

Scratching my head, I replied, "There's a lunch form?"

This time it was the lady from the lunchroom who rolled her eyes. "Yes, Sir, you have to send it in everyday so we will know how many of your students plan to eat lunch. Can I have yours, please?"

I looked at the students and hunched my shoulders. I didn't have a clue as to what a lunch form looked like. The children all started laughing.

Looking back at the lady from the lunchroom, who seemed to be getting a bit agitated with me, I asked, "Where do I find a lunch form? I'm kinda new here and haven't gotten the grasp of everything that a teacher has to do yet."

"It was in your box this morning. I put it in there myself yesterday afternoon. It should be with all the other things you got out of your box when you checked it this morning." The lunch lady stared at me. "You did check your box this morning, didn't you? Surely you know to do that! Everybody knows to do that!"

"He don't know much at all, Miz Boyd," Percival piped up, "'cause, axshally, he ain't no real techr, but I'll hep'em." Looking at me with his big blue eyes, Percival took charge. "I'll go git that form for ya', Techr. Ya' want me to git all the othur stuff, too?"

I nodded at Percival, stuck my hands in my pockets, and watched as the red-headed, freckled-faced, first grader proudly walked out the door and hurried to retrieve the "stuff" from my box. In no time at all, Percival was back. He handed me a stack of papers. I looked at the stack, wondering which one was the missing lunch form, when Percival motioned for me to lean down. I moved my head toward him, and he whispered in my ear, "It's the blue one, Techr."

I nodded to Percival and shuffled through the papers until I found the blue form. I glanced up at the children. "How many of you are eating lunch today?" Every hand went up except for one. I walked over to the little girl who did not raise her hand. "You're not eating, uh, what is your name?"

Two great, big, sad eyes looked back at me. The little girl shook her head and put it down on her arm that was resting on her desk. I quickly put the numbers on the blue form and handed it to the very impatient lady from the lunchroom. Percival had called her Mrs. Boyd. After a scalding look at me, Mrs. Boyd turned and scurried from my room.

I sighed and made a mental note that I would have to do something to redeem myself with Mrs. Boyd, or my servings at lunch would probably be a bit on the skimpy side.

The morning flew by rather quickly after that. Percival informed me when it was time to take bathroom breaks, stretch breaks, and every other kind of break he could think of to take. He also told me throughout the morning that I needed to hurry along and get to the next subject, or we'd be off schedule. With Percival's help, we managed to get in reading, health, and math before lunchtime. I also learned a few of the students' names, and that helped a lot. At least it kept Percival from yelling out the names every time I wanted to call on someone.

Taking twenty-one first graders to lunch proved to be an interesting and exhausting experience. After the children all washed their hands, they automatically lined up at the front of the room. Then they just stood there, looking at me. I looked back at them. "What? Why are you just standing there?" All in unison, the children made an "oohing" noise, and covered their mouths with their hands.

"What? Did I forget something?" I looked at Percival for help.

"Techr, this is when we say our blessin'. We ain't 'sposed to, but we do it anyway. 'Our other old 'Techr' said some big court judge said we ain't 'lowed to pray in school, but she said if we don't tell nobody and say it quiet like so's nobody can hear us but God, then it'll be okay."

I rolled my eyes upward. "'Techr' said that, eh? Well, if 'Techr' said it was all right, then it's okay with me, too. So, pray."

Another loud "ooh." "Ya' got to start it, Techr!" I frowned at Percival. I prayed a lot but not in front of people, especially twenty-one children. "I tell you what, Percival. You've been such a good helper today, why don't you lead the blessing."

I could tell by the smile on Percival's face that I'd finally done something right in his eyes. He got out of line and stood next to me with his hands behind his back. He started the "God is Great" prayer, and all the children said it quietly along with him. When they all said "Amen," Percival looked up at me. "Now we can go to lunch, Techr. Ya' want me to be the line leader?"

I smiled at Percival, and nodded my head. What a little guy! As much as he aggravated me, he was a natural born leader. His name should have been Sherman instead of Percival!

I followed the class to the lunchroom. I marveled at how each child knew exactly what to do. Of course, with a "line leader" like Percival, all they had to do was watch what he did.

After the children were all seated at the tables, I waited to get my plate. Mrs. Boyd handed it to me, and sure enough, it was skimpy! One little hotdog, about five baked beans, and half of a canned peach! I knew for certain that she was still holding a grudge about the blue lunch form. I also knew without a doubt that I'd be hungry before it was time to go home. I weakly smiled at her, and went to sit with the children.

The tables were all filled except for one where the little girl with the sad eyes was sitting. I sat down beside her. She looked over at my pitiful plate of food or what little there was of it. She let out a deep sigh, then turned and opened a small paper sack. She slowly took out a cold biscuit and a banana that was more the color of brown than yellow. She glanced back over at my plate and just kept staring at it. I lowered my head and looked her in the eyes. "What's your name?"

At first she didn't answer. I tried again. "What's your name?"

"Robin," a weak voice replied.

"Well, Robin, you know what?" I pointed to my lunch. "This is not at all what I wanted for lunch today. I tried to find a biscuit in my house this morning so I could bring it to eat, but all the biscuits were gone."

Robin looked down at her dry, over-cooked biscuit, then glanced back up at me.

"Why, Robin! You have just what I wanted for lunch! I don't suppose that you'd be willing to trade your biscuit for this old hotdog, now would you?"

Robin's sad eyes turned suddenly bright. She grabbed her sack, stuffed the old biscuit in it, and pushed it at me. "Ya' can have the banana, too, if ya' want it." Over came the much too ripe, brown banana.

I slid my plate across the table to Robin. After another quick smile at me, she dug into that hotdog. Chili and mustard went everywhere, including down the front of her faded, all ready stained shirt. In about three minutes flat, that "skimpy" plate of food was gone! With stains all over her impish little face, Robin looked at me. "Ya' better eat that biscuit fast now, Techr, 'cause we have to leave in a little bit."

I reached into the sack and took out the biscuit. I knew I had to eat it since those big green eyes were staring right at me. I quickly bit into the cold biscuit and choked it down in a hurry. "Don't forgit 'bout the banana, Techr. I gave it to ya', too."

Not the brown banana! But when I looked at Robin's expectant face, I knew I had to do it. I peeled that banana and stuffed it in my mouth before I could really get a good look at it. With the help of my glass of tea, I choked down the rottenest banana I have ever tasted. I must have been holding my breath when I felt Robin tugging at my sleeve. "Techr, ya' okay? Ya' had yore eyes shut and wuz makin' a awful face." I opened my eyes and looked at this dear child.

"Sure, I'm okay, Robin," I lied. "I was just thinking how much I love good bananas." Now that was the truth!

Percival walked up to me about that time, and whispered in my ear, "Techr, it's time for us to leave the lunchroom."

I looked at my line leader. "Thank you, Percival." We

left the lunch room a few minutes later, with Percival leading the way, and me following twenty first graders. Robin was not in line with the others. She was walking beside me holding my hand.

TEN

RIGHT AFTER LUNCH Percival informed me that it was time for recess. I thought it would be a breeze taking a group of children out to play, but no! First of all, I made a very grave error when I announced to the children it was time to go outside and play. They just sat and looked at me. I said in a louder, take charge voice, "So, go! What are you waiting for?"

All chaos broke loose then! In mass, all twenty-one children jumped up and ran out of the door. They were yelling and bumping into people, totally oblivious to anyone and anything that happened to get in their way. I ran behind them, yelling for them to stop and get in line, but those six-year-olds outran me by a long shot! They probably set a school record for reaching the playground faster than any group had ever done!

All of the other first grades were already out when my students stampeded onto the scene. In no time flat, children were screaming and crying and running to their teachers with tales of woe about what my class had done to them. I stared, wild-eyed, at the bedlam being created by the twenty-one very small people who were in my care.

I was still standing there looking when all four of the other first grade teachers stormed over to me. One particularly tight-lipped lady who probably should have retired at least ten years past, spoke first.

"Mr. Adams! Do something about your students this instant! They are acting like a bunch of hoodlums!"

Before I could answer, another teacher attacked. This one looked like she had eaten sour persimmons for lunch, her mouth was so pursed!

"You certainly have a lot to learn about how to deal with children, Young Man! I told the principal she was making a mistake when she hired you. Humph!" With that, the sour-faced first grade teacher threw back her head and held up one finger. Immediately, all twenty-one of her students ran quietly to get in the most perfect line I have ever seen. I watched in awe as they all but marched behind "Miss Sour Puss" into the building. It was days later that I found out that teacher's name. Miss Ida Mae Picklesimmer. The lady was an old maid who had been teaching first grade for twice as many years as I had been in the world, and she had been saddled with the name Ida Mae Picklesimmer. No wonder she always looked like she had been eating sour persimmons!

Frustration and embarrassment consumed me as I stood on the playground, taking the wrath of the other teachers. I stared at my feet and didn't say anything as angry words continued to be flung my way for what seemed like an eternity. Finally, I looked up to see that all but one teacher had stormed off the playground with their classes in tow.

"Don't feel so bad. They jumped on me just the same way when I first came here last year. All except for 'Miss Ellie.' I sure do miss her. I know you must miss her, too. I'm Anastasia Briggs. My room is in the portable classroom next to the music room. I also teach first grade."

My mouth dropped open as I quickly perused the person who had come to my defense. In the span of a few moments I took in a dark brown ponytail, a South Carolina sweatshirt, some baggy black pants, a pair of stained running shoes with broken shoelaces, and the largest, most beautiful, sparkling brown eyes that I had ever seen.

"Yeah, I sure do miss 'Techr.' I know she would have a thousand hissy fits if she could see what I have done to her class! But, thanks, anyway, for coming to my rescue, uh, Miss Briggs, did you say?"

"Anastasia. Just call me Anastasia. We all have to learn. It takes time. You'd die laughing if you could hear the things that happened to me last year. But I survived, and you will, too, Mr. Adams."

"Well, I don't plan to be around that long. I'm not really a teacher. I'm a medical student, or I was before 'Techr' died. I'm just trying to fill in until Mrs. Foster can find a suitable replacement. And, by the way, my name is Johnny."

Walking away to collect her kids, Anastasia looked back. "I know. See you later."

ELEVEN

ON MY WAY OUT of the school late that afternoon, I noticed that the other first grade teachers were congregated together at the end of the first grade wing. Miss Ida Mae Picklesimmer, who had her back turned away from me, was vehemently telling the others some sort of story when I walked by.

"He doesn't have a clue what to do, not a clue!" the matriarch of the first grade teachers ranted. "It's just embarrassing, that's what it is! Can you imagine what those kids are telling their parents about our school when they go home? My only hope is that God in His infinite wisdom will see fit to send us a decent teacher who'll know what to do with a class of first graders! And it can't be too soon, either! That boy is making a mockery out of the teaching profession! He doesn't belong here! He needs to go and do something he can do, like play baseball or Nintendo or whatever in the world he can do!"

Red with humiliation and sweating bullets, I strolled

casually by the group. "Have a nice, restful weekend, Ladies. I'd hang around and talk to you, but I have a lot to do...you know, baseball, Nintendo, and stuff. See you around!"

Miss Picklesimmer's head whipped around so fast that I swear I heard her neck crack! The others murmured something unintelligible and hurried off in different directions.

I walked as fast as my wobbly legs could carry me out of the building and up to the parking lot. It took me a few minutes to clear my head and remember what color rental car I had parked in the lot earlier that day. Gray? No, it was a putrid, mustard color. I walked over to the smallest car in the lot, a short, squatty little excuse for a car. I was taller than the car was long. I shook my head as I reached in my pocket for the key. I opened the door and folded my long legs under the steering wheel. I laid my head back with a loud groan. "What am I doing here? I can't teach; the kids think I'm stupid; the teachers want me gone; the lunchroom lady is starving me to death; a little freckled-faced, red-headed kid knows more about teaching than I do; and I'm driving a car that looks like a little squashed up jar of Gray Poupon. I feel like a long, skinny wiener, smothered in mustard!"

A gentle tapping on the window brought me out of my tirade of self pity. Without turning my head, my eyes caught the outline of someone at the window of the pathetic little car I had rented.

"Mr. Adams! Mr. Adams! Can I talk to you a minute?"

Reluctantly turning to face the voice, my eyes locked in on those bright, brown eyes again.

"Mr. Adams? Can you wait just a minute? Just a minute?" Anastasia with the big brown eyes looked plaintatively at me through the window. I reached for the automatic window button, only to discover there wasn't one. Frowning, I slowly rolled the window down.

I sighed and tilted my eyes backward as I looked into the face of one of the very same teachers I had seen standing around the Mouth of the South in the school just a few minutes earlier.

"Mr. Adams, don't feel badly about what you just heard in the hall. Ida Mae always has something to say about somebody. Don't take it personally." Anastasia's dark eyebrows took on a pleading look as she talked through the car window.

"Don't take it personally? I just struggled through two of the hardest days of my life with twenty-one six year olds, sniffling and crying and talking and wiggling, all at the same time, and I survived to tell about it, only to hear from my fellow teachers what a terrible teacher I am! Well, just for the record, 'Miss First Grade Teacher I Saw Standing With The Others,' Miss Picklesimmer is right on the money! I am NOT a teacher. I never WILL be a teacher, NOR do I WANT to be a teacher! I am a medical student, and I am going to be a doctor, just like my dad! Now would you kindly move out of the way so I can drive this little mustard jar, I mean car, out of this place! I have studying to do for a real profession!"

IF I had looked back, and IF I could have read lips, I would have seen Miss Anastasia Briggs with the big brown eyes saying, "Oh, you'll be a teacher all right, Mr. Adams. You just wait and see! It's already in your blood! You're just like me! You'll be a teacher!"

But I didn't look back. I was too busy planning my weekend to give that school or that teacher a thought.

TWELVE

BY THE TIME I REACHED the car rental place that had suckered me into probably the worst excuse for a car in the entire universe, I was hopping mad. But I had a plan. First, I had to get rid of that ugly car. Then, I was going to head to 'Techr's' house, call the principal and get rid of my "temporary" teacher's position. Heck, I'd lasted two whole days. Maybe I'd set some kind of record for the shortest teaching career in history! Then, I was going to grab me a cold root beer, order a pizza with double meat and double cheese, and hit the books. I had some serious cramming to do since my midterm exams were right around the corner.

When I headed for the phone, I noticed the red button blinking. Thinking it was probably the latest in a long line of urgent messages from my dad, I hit the retrieve button. It was the principal. I eased down in the old worn chair beside the phone and listened.

"Johnny, this is Shelli Foster. I sincerely hope you hear this message soon. Johnny, I have some really bad news!

After everyone left the school this afternoon, I got a call from a lady who lives beside little Robin Carroll's house. You know, the little girl in your class who always brings her lunch to school? Well, the neighbor heard a terrible commotion at Robin's house this afternoon. She looked through her curtains, to see what was going on when she saw little Robin run out of the house and hide behind one of the big oak trees in the backyard. There's more, Johnny, that I can't leave on your answering machine. Call me! The number is 543-2001. I'm with Robin now, but I think she needs you, Johnny! Please call!"

"Oh, God, no! Not Robin with the sad eyes! Not Robin who held my hand today! Please, God, let her be okay!" I continued to pray as my trembling fingers dialed the number Mrs. Foster had left on the message.

After one short ring, a very old voice spoke into the phone. "H'lo, this here's Gertrude speakin'. Can I hep' ya'?"

"Uh, this is Johnny Adams. I must have the wrong number. I was looking for Mrs. Foster."

"No, Young Man. Ya' got the right place. Miz Foster is here. Let me git her fer ya'."

My heart raced as I waited for the principal to get on the line. "Johnny! I'm so glad you got my message! Oh, Johnny! You won't believe what has happened to little Robin." Mrs. Foster's voice broke as she tried to speak.

"Please come over here, Johnny. I can't get through to the child. I saw you with her in the lunchroom today, and I thought maybe you could talk to her."

"What happened, Mrs. Foster? Is Robin hurt?" All sorts of images were flying through my mind.

"Johnny, I can't tell you on the phone. Just come. I really need you. Please!"

"Okay, Mrs. Foster. I'll have to call a cab. Where to, Mrs. Foster?"

"It's an old house right behind the YMCA. It's the third house on the left. The paint used to be white, but it's mostly brown and peeling now. My car is in the front, Johnny. I drive a green, Chevy van. Hurry, Johnny! I really need you!"

With a thousand questions mulling through my brain, I started to call for a taxi, when I thought of 'Techr's' old brown sedan out in her garage. I remembered seeing the keys hanging on a hook in the kitchen. I ran through the house, grabbed the keys, and hurried to the garage.

There it sat. The old, dilapidated monster that 'Techr' had driven back and forth to school for more years than I could remember. "Okay, Baby! 'Techr's' gone, and I'm here! I really need you to be kind to me today."

I rammed the key into the ignition and turned. Nothing. "Come on, Baby! Crank! You did it for 'Techr' everyday when she needed you, now do it for me! Come on, Baby!" I turned the key again. Nothing. I guess I lost it then. I beat on the faded, cracked dash, shook the steering wheel, and yelled to the top of my lungs. "Crank, you sorry, ugly old piece of junk!" I turned the key again, and much to my surprise, the old car sputtered to life. I looked around to see if anyone was watching. Then I leaned over and planted a big sloppy kiss on the dashboard of that old car. "Thank you, old car."

Now anyone who saw us that day, that is, the old brown Chrysler sedan and me, would have thought that we belonged together. We were a pair, flying through the streets together. In about ten minutes flat, I pulled up behind Mrs. Foster's shiny, green van.

I sat there a minute and looked at the house. It was indeed old with moldy shutters hanging from the windows. Most of the paint had peeled away from the outside walls, and the roof had a battered and worn look. There was a porch that wrapped around the old house with uneven boards jutting out in all directions.

But the thing that struck me the most was that the house, as worn as it was, looked clean! No clutter was visible on the porch, and the front yard had actually been swept. The broom marks in the clay-packed dirt obviously had just been freshly made.

About fifty yards down the street on the left side sat a house trailer. It was nestled in weeds that had grown to over five feet tall. The windows and the door of the trailer were standing open, and there was no evidence of screens anywhere. Loud country music was wafting through the open windows.

I finally broke from my perusal of the area and got out of the car. As I approached the steps to the old house, a lady appeared at the front door. She must have been at least ninety years old. She was bent at the waist and had a huge dowager's hump on her back. Her hair was snow white, her face was ebony black, and she didn't have a tooth in her head. Wiping her hands on her old faded apron, she opened the screen door. "Come on in, Young Fella. Ya' must be Johnny. I'm Gertrude. That principal lady's in yonder."

Gertrude pointed to a back room. I nodded at her and walked slowly in the direction she was pointing. I had to adjust my eyes to the darkness as I entered the room. I felt a warm hand on my shoulder, and I jerked quickly. It was Mrs. Foster.

"Wha..?" I started to ask. Mrs. Foster gently put her finger to my mouth to shush me and pointed to the corner. Huddled in a heap with her arms over her head was little Robin. I quietly walked over to her and knelt down. The little form was as still as death, and I really couldn't see her head at all.

"Robin? Robin?" I said softly. "It's Mr. Adams, your teacher from school." There was no response. The little lump in the corner didn't move.

"Robin? Can you hear me? Look at me if you can hear me. Okay? I'm here to help you. Robin?"

Very slowly two green eyes peered out from under the folded arms. "Techr? I'm sorry I wuz bad."

The look in those sad green eyes tore me apart. "Robin, Honey, come here and talk to me. Please tell me what happened."

After a few agonizing minutes Robin put her arms down and turned to face me. I had a sudden intake of breath as I stared at this precious child. She was completely bald!

For a few moments I was speechless! Then I reached over and carefully put my hands on Robin's little slumping shoulders. "Who did this to you, Robin? Who?"

Robin's head dropped. She didn't answer.

I leaned down and looked straight into her sad little eyes. "Tell me, Robin. Who shaved your head? You can tell me, Robin. I'm here to help you."

It seemed like an eternity before I heard Robin's timid little voice answer. "Daddy. Daddy did it 'cause I wuz bad."

I had to choke back my anger, and yes, my tears, too. "What did you do that was bad, Robin?"

"I spilled my drink in Daddy's car. He told me not to spill it, and I did. I didn't mean to…it jest slipped outta my hand. I'm sorry I wuz bad, Techr." Robin looked at me with those big sad eyes, and I really lost it then. Tears spilled out of my eyes as I watched that poor, precious child. She was so thin, so pale, not a hair on her head, and not a tear in her eyes. I enfolded her in my strong arms and wept like a baby.

I felt a small hand on my face. I pulled away from Robin only to see that she was trying to comfort me. "Don't cry, Techr. It'll grow back. It always duz. 'Specially if I'm not bad no more."

I couldn't stand it. I was furious! I took Robin's little shoulders in my big hands and held her. "Robin, you are not bad! Everybody spills things. I even spill things. That doesn't mean you're bad!" Robin looked away. I gently turned her face back to me. "Listen, Robin, you are not bad. What your daddy did to you is bad. And we're going to help you. Mrs. Foster and me. We'll get you some help so this won't ever happen to you again!"

"No! You can't tell! No! Don't tell nobody. Daddy said I can't tell!" Robin grabbed my face with both of her little hands. "Please, Techr! Don't tell nobody. I promise I'll be good! Jest don't tell nobody!"

I glanced around at Mrs. Foster. She shrugged her shoulders and nodded at me. I rubbed my hand over Robin's slick little head. "Okay, Robin. Okay. We won't tell if that's what you want. Okay?"

Robin slowly got to her feet. "Thank ya', Techr. I gotta go now, 'cause Daddy's going to start to wonderin' where I am. I gotta hurry, or Daddy'll be mad agin." With that, Robin ran out of the house and headed back to the broken-down trailer down the street.

I watched from the door of Gertrude's house as Robin quietly slipped in the open door of the old trailer that was hidden in the weeds. The loud music continued to bellow from the trailer, and I only had to guess and hope that little Robin had entered without being noticed.

Dropping my head, and without a word to Mrs. Foster or Gertrude, I walked out of the front door and got in 'Techr's' old brown car. I don't remember cranking the car or driving home. All I remember is a heavy sad feeling that wouldn't go away.

THIRTEEN

WHEN I TRY TO PUT together the rest of that weekend, it seems hazy and out of focus. I really can't remember what I did. I do remember some things I did not do. I did not study for my midterms; I did not call the principal and quit my job; I did not order pizza with extra cheese; and I did not sleep. I was totally numb, and my every thought was about a little sad-eyed girl with a shaved head and a broken spirit.

On Sunday afternoon, I did go to a convenience store nearby and purchase a pink stocking cap for my little friend to wear over her shaved head. The last thing I wanted was for the other children in the school to laugh and poke fun at her.

Monday was a cold, blustery day. I listened to the weather forecast on the car radio as I drove the little brown sedan to school. A possibility of snow flurries was predicted for later that day. "Not likely," I said to myself. "Not in this little southern town in the middle of nowhere."

I drove on in silence and arrived at the school even before the custodians got there to open the building.

Hunkered down in my unlined windbreaker and Atlanta Braves ball cap, I headed for the entrance where the buses unloaded the children each day. I knew Robin rode a bus to school, and I wanted to be there when she got off the bus.

After about fifteen minutes of shivering in the cold, another teacher came through the door to assume her position on early morning bus duty. "Morning," I said without looking up to see who was standing beside me.

"What're you doing out here?" a prickly voice replied. I rolled my eyes back in my head as I recognized that voice. Miss Picklesimmer, no less! Of all the people who could have been on bus duty that particular morning, it just had to be Miss Picklesimmer.

"Just helping out, Miss Picklesimmer," I replied in a cheerful voice. "Just helping out. A little chilly this morning, isn't it?"

After a loud sigh, the old, seasoned, first grade teacher standing beside me replied, "Well, if you had sense enough to wear some warm clothes instead of that flimsy jacket you've got on, maybe you wouldn't be so cold. I don't know why you're out here anyway. It's my turn today, and I don't need any help. Why don't you go on back in the building and try to get yourself organized for the day. Heaven knows you need to get ready!"

I was about to tell that old biddy where she could go when the first bus rolled up to the school. I quickly forgot my anger as the children started pouring down the steps of the bus. Most of them were huddled up in coats, so I had to look at each one carefully in order to spot little Robin. But she wasn't on that bus.

Robin wasn't on the next five buses either. I was about to give up and go to my room when the final bus rolled in. The children filed off, laughing and excited about the impending snow. Then I saw her. Robin. She slowly walked down the steps, with one hand on the school bus railing, and the other hand holding a ratty, oversized coat over her head. I walked over to her and put my arm around her slender shoulders. She leaned into me just a bit, and we walked through the door of the school. Just inside, I stopped and knelt down in front of Robin. I reached inside my pocket and pulled out the little, pink stocking cap. "Here, Robin, this is for you."

Those sad, green eyes looked out from under the big coat, as a timid little hand reached for the cap. "Thank you, Techr," the small girl said quietly as she pushed back the unsightly coat and placed the pink cap on her little bald head.

We walked to our room then, like nothing was wrong. When Robin entered the class, several of the children still had on stocking caps, so she fit right in. And that day, I didn't remind a single child to remove a cap or hat.

So day three of my teaching career had begun.

FOURTEEN

ABOUT TEN O'CLOCK that morning there was a knock on my classroom door. At the time I was in the back of the room working with a reading group. Actually, it was Robin's group. She had her little plastic, molded chair right next to my leg and her head hidden behind her reading book. Percival hurried to answer the door.

"Techr, it's the principal and that other lady here to see ya'." I frowned as I looked up at the intruders.

"Thank you, Percival." I motioned with my head for my red-headed helper to take his seat. "Boys and girls, look at the pictures on the next page and sit quietly until I get back." The group in the reading circle nodded quietly.

I walked over to the door with a puzzled look on my face.

"Can we talk in the hall a minute, Mr. Adams?" the principal said solemnly. I stepped outside the door and folded my arms against my chest.

"Johnny, this is Mary Sinclair. She's from the

Department of Social Services. She needs to talk to Robin."

I glared at the principal, my heart racing ninety miles a minute! "You called DSS? But we promised her, Mrs. Foster! Why did you do that?"

"I had to call, Johnny. It's the law. I know you promised Robin that we wouldn't tell, but I have to report any suspected child abuse. I had to, Johnny. I didn't have a choice. Now please get Robin so Ms. Sinclair can find out what really happened to her yesterday. Oh, and Johnny, she'll need to get some pictures, too."

I couldn't believe what I was hearing! I stared in total disbelief at the principal and shook my head. "Please, no, Mrs. Foster! She's been through enough already. She's calm right now, and she trusts me! Please don't do this to her!"

"I have to, Johnny. It's the law! Now, please get her!"

After several moments of staring at Mrs. Foster in frustration and despair, I turned and walked slowly back into the classroom. Apparently the children had heard some of the conversation in the hall, because they were all sitting like stones when I entered the room. With lead feet, I walked to the back of the room and touched Robin on the shoulder.

"Robin, there is a nice lady at the door who wants to talk to you for a little while. Will you go and talk to her?" Robin's little head, encased in the pink stocking cap, looked around at me. She didn't say a word, but her sad eyes spoke volumes. I had betrayed her trust, just like everybody else in her young life. Without taking her eyes from me, she got up from her small, plastic chair and walked slowly out of the room. I just stood there and watched with a huge lump in my throat and my heart breaking into a thousand pieces. A sick feeling crept over my entire body.

I felt a small tapping on my leg and looked down to see Percival looking up at me. "Don't worry, Techr. Robin'll be back t'reckly. She has to go talk to that lady a lot, but she always comes back."

Robin did come back after what seemed to be an eternity to me. She went straight to her desk and put her head down on her arm. I tried to talk to her, but she wouldn't answer. At lunch, I sat with her and offered to trade lunches again, but she just ignored me as she ate her cold biscuit.

Right after lunch it started snowing. The children got so excited as they watched their little southern town turn into a winter wonderland. They laughed and chattered and couldn't stay away from the windows. All but Robin. She just sat at her desk with her head down, staring off into space.

The crackling of the intercom got everyone's attention. It was Mrs. Foster's voice. "Teachers! Boys and Girls! Due to the snow and the road conditions, school will be letting out early today. Please prepare to dismiss immediately. The buses should be arriving in about twenty minutes. Have a safe trip home, and be sure to listen to your radios and TV's about openings and closings tomorrow."

The children went wild! They ran to the back of the room and started putting on their coats and hats, all the while laughing and talking and jumping around. All but Robin. She just sat in her desk with her head down. I walked over to her and touched her on the shoulder. She didn't pull away. She just turned those enormous green eyes towards me.

"Robin, Honey. It's time to go home. Go get your coat so the bus won't leave you. Okay?"

Obediently, Robin got out of her desk and walked to the back of the room. She pulled the old ratty coat from the hook and slipped her small arms into the long sleeves. She turned and came back to where I was standing. Looking up at me with those drooping eyes, she quietly slipped the little pink stocking cap off of her bald head and handed it to me. She than pulled the big coat over her slick head and went to line up with the other children.

The buses were called at that moment, and Robin walked out of my classroom, huddled under the old ratty coat. I almost chased after her to give her the pink cap back, but I didn't. I knew she couldn't wear it home. And she knew, too. Her little head had to be uncovered and bald for the world to see when she stepped off that bus at home.

I never saw little Robin again. She didn't come back to school. Her family disappeared into thin air, and was never heard of again. Oh, the school, the police department and the Department of Social Services all searched diligently for them, but that abusive, horrible, sorry daddy covered his tracks well.

I kept the little pink stocking cap. I framed it and put it over the nightstand in 'Techr's' old house. Every time I look at it, I remember Robin, the little girl with the big, sad eyes and the bald head, and I pray that somehow, someway, she found some peace and love in her life. I guess I'll never know.

FIFTEEN

IT SNOWED LIKE CRAZY for the next two days, and the thermometer hovered around the freezing mark. The power went out in 'Techr's' old house during the early morning hours of the second day of the snow. I piled on several layers of clothes and went out back to search for something that would burn in the fireplace.

The backyard was solid white, so I headed around the side of the house and rummaged through the garage for a while. I noticed a large black tarp over in one corner with something bulky piled under it. I managed to drag the cold, stiff canvas over towards me, and what I found underneath the old thing made me laugh out loud.

Stacked in the most unsightly pile I had ever seen was a large, unevenly cut, bunch of firewood. 'Techr!' Even in her death, she was still looking out for me! My eyes looked Heavenward, and I mouthed a silent "Thank You!"

I quickly gathered up as many of those roughly hewn logs as my arms could hold and headed for the house. My

Boy Scout training came in handy that day. In just a few minutes I had a roaring fire crackling in the ancient, smoke-encrusted fireplace. I pulled 'Techr's' old rocker up close to the fire and stretched my long legs out to warm.

"Okay, Johnny, what now?" I asked out loud to myself. My strongest urge at that moment was just to sit and stare at the roaring blaze in the fireplace. But that only added to my despair over little Robin, and I knew moping about wouldn't change anything where she was concerned. I really needed to hit the books and study for the tests I had coming up in just a few days. But I didn't want to do that either. I couldn't watch TV since the power was out. I didn't know what to do.

In the end, I reluctantly got out the notes my friend had sent me from school, and started to pour over them. Ironically, one of the courses I was currently enrolled in was Pediatric Development and Care. As I thumbed through the notes about children, I quickly passed over to the section on six to seven year olds. Vivid pictures formed in my mind when I read the part about six year olds losing their baby teeth. I suddenly saw Pat as plain as if he were standing in front of me! The beautiful little blonde-headed, blue-eyed boy on the second row, third seat back. He had one big, white permanent tooth in the front of his mouth and one, large gaping hole where the other one had not even begun to grow. Then there was Malcolm, on the third row, back seat. How funny he looked and sounded with both of his front teeth missing. I chuckled as I thought about how he pronounced my name, something like

'Mithur Adamth.'

Before I knew it, the morning had slipped away. The grumbling in my stomach told me that I had missed lunch. I put the notes down beside my chair and went into the kitchen to find something to eat. As I finished off the last bite of a triple-decker peanut butter, jelly, and mayonnaise sandwich, the telephone rang.

"Hetho," I mumbled through the glob of peanut butter that was stuck to the roof of my mouth. There was a brief moment of silence on the other end of the line.

"Johnny? Is that you? You sound kind of funny."

My heart sank as I heard Dad's voice on the line. I knew I was in for lecture number 1003! "It's me, Dad. Sorry, I was just finishing a sandwich. How're you doing?"

"Well, Johnny, I think I should ask you that question. Why in Heaven's name are you still at 'Techr's' house? Aren't your midterms this Friday?"

I had to think fast. "Yes, Sir, they are, and I've been studying up a storm for them." I looked down at my crossed fingers and hoped God wouldn't strike me dead for the little white lie. I had been studying…today…while the power was off, and the snow was falling outside. I knew all there was to know about six year olds losing their baby teeth!

I heard Dad clear his throat. "Well, Johnny, why aren't you back at the university instead of still in South Carolina?"

"Uh, Dad, you won't believe this, but I've been helping out with 'Techr's' class for the last few days."

"You're what? Johnny! Why on Earth are you doing that? You're not a teacher!"

Boy! I was really getting tired of people telling me that! Through clenched teeth, I tried to explain. "Dad, the principal, Mrs. Foster, uh, I think you met her at the funeral, well...she called me last week and asked me if I could fill in for 'Techr' until she could find a replacement. Since I was here and all, and since 'Techr's' students were scattered all over the school in different rooms, I decided I owed it to 'Techr' to help out for a few days. I figured you'd want me to do that for 'Techr', Dad!"

I heard the catch in Dad's throat as he replied, "Uh, Johnny, that's real noble of you, and I'm proud that you want to help." Then Dad's voice took on the confident air that I was so used to hearing. "But, Johnny, let me repeat! You are NOT a teacher! You are a medical student who has midterms in two days! Now listen carefully because I'm only going to tell you this one time! Johnny! I am putting a one way ticket in overnight express mail for you to return to Georgia. You'd better be on that plane, Son! And, one more thing! I will accept nothing lower than a 'B' on those midterms!" Click! The line went dead.

I held the phone for a few minutes while the monotone of the dial tone reverberated in my ear. I finally placed the receiver on its cradle and stared back at the fire. The crackling of the burning embers suddenly broke the silence in the still, dark room.

Slowly I rose to my feet and walked over to the window. As I watched the snow pile higher on the old cedar tree in the front yard, I knew what I had to do. I should have seen it many years ago. It was as plain as the nose on my face; like an open roadmap of the turns and intersections that my life was to take. I knew at that moment I didn't have a choice. It was my destiny!

SIXTEEN

THE ONSET OF YET another headache threatened as I stretched out my long legs in the rather roomy seat of Flight 221, the red-eye to Atlanta. How like Dad to send me a first class ticket. That was him. Nothing but the best for his son, in spite of the fact that the flight was only one way.

I thought back to the day I had just spent at school. The children had dwindled in throughout the morning since so many parents didn't want their babies on the buses with pockets of snow still on the roads. I can't say that I could blame them.

All day I waited for Robin to walk through the door. But she never came. Her little desk sat blatantly bare, and by the end of the day, I found that I could not even look back at it. I tried to teach some and follow the schedule for Thursday, but I'm afraid I didn't do a whole lot of quality teaching. The excitement of the children coupled with my despondent attitude, made for a generally wasted day. I was glad to see the day come to an end.

Mrs. Foster had seemed okay with me taking Friday off to go and take my midterms. I figured I'd call her later from Athens and drop the bomb that I wouldn't be back. I knew that was the sensible thing to do. To not ever go back, that is.

Everybody was right! I wasn't a teacher! Those kids needed more than a big, stupid klutz like me to teach them. And I didn't need all that stress, either! Why in the world would I want to put up with sniffly kids who talked all the time; bossy, know-it-all kids, with red, kinky hair who DID know it all; old gossipy teachers who talked about you; and sad-eyed, hungry little girls with bald heads? And for what? Teacher's pay? I doubted it was enough to even pay the taxes on the new BMW that Dad's doctor's pay had bought me for my last birthday!

I hated to admit it, but Dad was right for a change! I should be a doctor, not a teacher for Heaven's sake! Who in the world in their right mind would ever want to be a teacher?

I settled back in the comfy, first class seat, closed my tired eyes, and tried to picture myself in a white doctor's coat with my own personal nametag pinned on the left breast pocket – Dr. Johnny Adams. The picture I kept trying to conjure up in my mind seemed cloudy and distorted as I dropped off to sleep.

SEVENTEEN

AFTER STRUGGLING THROUGH four pretty tough exams, the last one seemed like a breeze. I knew every answer! I chuckled to myself when I read the final essay question. *Describe, in detail, the growth and development pattern of a six year old child.*

A sign from God! That's what it had to be! With a crystal, clear vision of twenty-one…no twenty… first graders, I quickly described the most colorful and energetic six year old ever imagined. When I proofed my finished masterpiece for errors, I realized that I had created a perfect composite of the children in 'Techr's' class, from Pat's missing front tooth to Percival's red hair and freckles.

Swaggering to the point of being boastful, I flicked my paper down on the desk where the professor was sitting and looked at him with what could only be described as a smirk. He looked up at me, puzzled by my sudden change of attitude. But he didn't know. He would never know that his test had changed my life forever.

Hurrying down the steps of the old, hallowed building that had produced so many fine doctors over the last century and beyond, I glanced at my watch. It was already 5:45 in the afternoon. My pace quickened, and I was all but running when I entered the ivy covered, green building where I had lived for the past couple of years. My old buddies greeted me enthusiastically with lots of backslapping and high fives, and I responded in kind, all the while taking in the beer cans and cigarette butts scattered in disarray throughout the room.

"How ya' been doing, Buddy," the number one beer guzzler of the group asked, in a slurred voice. "You want a beer?"

"No thanks, Joe." Apparently Joe had forgotten that I didn't drink. I thought they all knew the story about my dad and his alcoholic parents. Heck, if Tara or I had ever touched a drop of the stuff, Dad would have disowned us!

Looking around at the guys who had been my closest buddies, I knew they deserved an explanation. "Fellows, it's been kind of tough for me the last couple of weeks. You know my grandmother in South Carolina died, and my family and I went out to her funeral. Well, she had been a teacher, uh, a first grade teacher, and, uh, when she died right in the middle of the school year, there wasn't anyone to teach her students." I looked around at the guys. They were staring at me in disbelief!

"You didn't! Tell us you didn't take over her teacher's job?" This time it was Lynn, the lady's man.

I nodded my head up and down, biting on my lower lip

while I waited for the response I knew, without a doubt, was coming.

Nothing. None of my friends in the room said a word. Not even Joe with his belly bulging with beer.

Before I knew it, I was pouring out the stories about the children in 'Techr's' class. They guffawed when they heard about Percival, and they didn't make a sound, except for a sniffle or two, as I quietly told them about Robin and her little bald head.

When finally, I stopped to catch a breath, I looked at my friends, with the threat of tears welling up in my eyes. "I have to go back, fellows. Those little people need me, and I think I need them, too. I have to go back. But I can't tell my dad…not yet, anyway. He'll kill me!" I reached inside my pockets and turned them inside out. "And this is what I have…nothing. Not even enough money to buy a return ticket back. I don't know what to do! I don't have time to drive all the way back. I have to fly so I can get back in a hurry!"

That's when Tommy, the con man, walked over and put his arm around my shoulders. "I tell you what, Johnny. I think I've got a solution. You leave your car for us to use for our hottest dates. You know, when we need to make really good impressions, and we'll chip in and buy you that plane ticket. Heck, we might just throw in a few extra bucks for a burger or two! How's that sound to you?"

A mental picture of those guys driving my car, my most prized possession, almost made me change my mind about going back. But then I thought of the kids, and I nodded in agreement. "Okay, Tommy, it's a deal. But, let it be known! If anyone of you so much as puts a finger smudge on my car, then I will be back to haunt you. Clear?"

I've never seen money come out of pockets so fast. One after another the guys pressed bills into my hands, until I couldn't hold anymore. Then they deserted me as if I wasn't in the room. They had gone to make out a schedule for the use of my car.

I don't think the guys even heard me when I called the airport or slipped out the door to get in the cab. It didn't matter. I was going back...back to 'Techr's' house...back to the little town that seemed like home to me...and back to my class of first graders with the sniffly noses, wiggly bodies, little kid odors, and irritating voices. I was so excited!

EIGHTEEN

I SLEPT IN SATURDAY MORNING. My old bed at 'Techr's' house felt like a little piece of Heaven after my whirlwind trip to the university and back. It was nearly twelve noon when the shrill ringing of the phone awakened me from my near semi-conscious state. Numbly, I reached over and picked up the receiver.

"Hello," I mumbled.

There was no answer.

"Hello?" I repeated, a little louder this time.

"Mr. Adams? This is Anastasia Briggs. You know, the teacher you told off the other day in the parking lot?"

"Miss Briggs? Sorry 'bout that. I was pretty upset that afternoon."

"That's okay, Mr. Adams. I understand. Uh, I was just calling to check on you since you weren't at school yesterday. Are you all right?"

"Oh, yeah, sure. I'm okay. Just had to go take some midterms back in Georgia. But I'm a little surprised to hear from you. How did you know I wasn't at school yesterday, you being out in that portable building and all?"

The voice on the other end of the line laughed. "Well, since I had twenty extra little bodies in my class for the day, I somehow figured you weren't around!"

"You had them all?" I couldn't believe what I was hearing.

"Yes, I did. But it's okay. They were really good, and Percival helped me more than you will ever know!"

"Good old Percival to the rescue, eh? I hope you let him know right off who was the boss." I laughed, and it really felt good.

"Well, it was established early on who the boss would be, and it definitely was not me!" The giggle in the phone let me know that Miss Briggs did not hold any grudges against me. Actually, she sounded downright friendly.

"Well, I've gotta run, Johnny. I have so much to do today. I'm glad you're okay. See you Monday!"

Johnny? She called me Johnny? In the true form of a major klutz, I answered, "Yeah, uh, see you Monday. Thanks for calling."

The click on the other end let me know the call had been disconnected. I held the phone to my ear for another few seconds before slowly putting it down. Johnny?

Puzzled and a little more than confused, I got out of bed and walked to the window. The sun was shinning on the few remaining patches of snow that refused to melt away. I felt so happy I started singing! It was a truly beautiful day! An absolutely beautiful day!

NINETEEN

MONDAY HERALDED the first day of March in true form. The wind whipped 'Techr's' old Chrysler all over the place as I drove to school.

When I pulled into the parking lot, I laughed out loud. I was the second one to arrive, so I had my pick of the parking spaces. Did I dare take Ida Mae Picklesimmer's spot? Why not? She already hated me.

So, brassy as a soldier's belt buckle, I whipped into the first space, the one closest to the building. After locking the car door, I headed toward the building. "So there, Miss Sourpuss!" I spouted, brazenly, with a look of contempt on my clean-shaven face. "All I can say is that you have to get here real early to get a good parking place!" Whistling a jaunty tune, I walked briskly against the surging wind toward the building.

"Morning, Miss Merle. Beautiful day, isn't it?" The devoted custodian, who had been at the school for more years than I had been in the world, stopped sweeping the hall and stared at me.

"You here mighty early, Mr. Adams. You okay?"

I stopped and draped my arm around the portly shoulders of that wonderful lady. "Well, you know what they say, Miss Merle. The early bird gets the worm. However, in this case, the early bird gets the best parking place!"

Slapping her hands together, Miss Merle's dark face broke into a million dollar smile. "Now ain't that the truth, Mr. Adams. That sure is the truth. Good day to park close, too, in my way of thinking, with that wind and all."

"It sure is, Miss Merle. It sure is. Now you have a wonderful day, you hear?" I gave that sweet lady my best smile and headed on down to my room. I could sense that she was staring at me as I walked away, and I knew, without a doubt, that I had just captured the best friend I could ever have in the school. Well, just about, except for the lady in the lunchroom. I knew I still had some work to do there if I was ever going to get enough to eat!

By the time the children arrived, I was standing at the door of the classroom, with my hands behind my back, trying to look like I knew what I was doing. My heart swelled with pride when my little first graders came trooping into the class.

"Hey, Techr!" "Morning, Techr!" "How ya' doin,' Sir?" "Well, hey, Mither Adamth!" "Mornin', Techr." "Hello, Mr. Techr." "Hey, Teduh!" "You back agin?" That was Percival! Most of the others just looked up at me and smiled. One girl with straight, reddish-blonde hair and huge blue eyes reached over and slipped her tiny hand in mine. I racked my brain to think of her name. I knew it started with an "M." Squeezing her hand, I ventured a guess. "Good morning, uh, Meredith?" The blue eyes got bigger as the little tyke shook her head. "Mary Anne?"

"Nope."

Bending over to look the little girl square in the eyes, I asked, "Well, what is your name, Sweetie?"

"Not gonna tell ya'." With that she pulled her hand from mine and sauntered to her desk. I hurried over to my desk and looked at the list of names in the grade book. There it was! Madalyn! I remembered then!

Casually, I walked around the room while I checked the roll. When I called Madalyn's name, I stopped and looked straight at her. Her impish face broke into a great big smile, and she quickly ducked her pretty little blonde head under her arms.

"Well, it looks like everyone's here." I smiled at the children with an air of confidence I hadn't felt since I had been there. From the back of the room a voice spoke up.

"Cept for Robin. She ain't here."

My air of confidence left immediately. Finally allowing my eyes to venture over to Robin's empty desk, I answered, "No. No, she's not." After a prolonged moment of silence, I managed to speak in a quivery voice. "Well, let's get on with our morning work, boys and girls." I silently vowed right then and there to have that desk removed at the end of the day. I couldn't bear to look at it.

TWENTY

THE CLASS HAD JUST returned from music and settled down to finish their math seatwork when there was a knock at the door. Percival jumped up to go to the door, but I motioned for him to sit back down and complete his work. With an ugly old frown on his face, he returned to his seat. I walked over and opened the door.

Mrs. Foster was standing there, holding the hand of a little boy I had never seen.

"Mr. Adams. I seem to have a problem. This little fellow came in on one of the buses this morning, and I'm not sure what to do with him. One of the other children who came in on the same bus told me that the boy lives in a duplex over on Second Street. Just by looking at him, I'm guessing that he is probably a first grader. So I'm going to put him in your class for the time being until I can find out something about him."

I looked down at the black, curly headed young boy who was standing facing me. He smiled and waved his little hand. "Well, hello, young fellow. What is your name?"

The little boy's smile widened. "M'tus Doan."

I glanced up at the principal. "What's that? What is your name?"

An even wider smile. "M'tus Doan."

I looked back at Mrs. Foster. She shrugged her shoulders and shook her head. "I can't understand him either. Nobody can. Try asking him how old he is."

Kneeling down in front of the little fellow, I looked straight into his dark brown eyes. "So, Buddy! How old are you?"

The shiny brown face broke into another wide smile. "Be tic be'r doad!" The little tyke shook his head up and down, smiling proudly, at this revelation!

"See what I mean?" Mrs. Foster mouthed quietly to me. "So, if you will please keep him in your class for the rest of the day, I'll take him home right after school and try to find out some information from his mother."

I glanced at the boy, then leaned over and whispered in the principal's ear. "What do I call him?"

"Your guess is as good as mine!" Mrs. Foster winked at me, turned and walked away.

With a feeling of helplessness, I reached down and took the little boy's chubby hand in mine. "Come on, Little Buddy. I just happen to have an empty desk waiting for you," and I led the boy to Robin's recently vacated desk.

The other children quietly watched as Child X took his seat in the empty desk.

Knowing I had to say something, I announced, "Boys and girls! This is, uh, Buddy."

The children stared at the new boy. "Buddy" looked back at them and smiled broadly. "Be dame M'tus Doan, dot Duh De." The children stared even harder. Then good old Percival got out of his desk and walked over to the new kid. He leaned over and looked him squarely in the eyes.

"You from France?"

"Buddy" smiled back at Percival. "Do, be dame M'tus Doan!"

For a brief instant, Percival frowned at the boy. Then he turned to the class. "Yep, this boy's from France." And with that profound announcement, Percival took his seat and continued his work.

It was a long day. Oh, "Buddy" was no trouble. He just sat in Robin's desk most of the time and smiled. But I was nervous as a cat, because I couldn't communicate with him. I was really glad when the day came to an end.

When all the other children had gone, I took "Buddy" by the hand and walked down to the office. After glancing in Mrs. Foster's office and finding it empty, I took a seat on the couch in the waiting area. "Buddy" sat right beside me, about as close as he could get.

"You waiting to see Mrs. Foster?" the secretary asked after a few minutes.

I nodded my head.

"Well, she won't be back today. She was called to the district office for a meeting."

I jumped up. "What am I supposed to do with this little boy then? Mrs. Foster said she was going to try to find his mother so we can figure out who he is!"

"Sorry," Sheila, the secretary replied. "She must've forgotten. Guess you'll have to take him home."

Abruptly, I sucked in a huge gulp of air and started coughing. This was impossible! The more I panicked, the more I coughed! Then I felt a slight tug on my shirt sleeve.

"Do doe-tay, de-dah?" With a break in the coughing, I turned my attention to the small child beside me. That's when I knew I had to do something. I stood up and took the boy's hand.

"Come on, Buddy. Let's see if we can find where you live." The small brown hand clasped mine tightly, and we headed out the door. Miss Merle stopped sweeping and propped on the long broom handle. I raised my hand at her, waving good bye, when I suddenly had a brilliant idea.

"Miss Merle, want to go for a little ride?"

"What you mean, Mister Adams? I've got work to do."

Grimacing, I whined, "Miss Merle, I really could use your help. I've got to take my little buddy here home, and I don't know where he lives. Plus, I've never done this before. I sure could use your help. Please?"

Propping the wide broom in the corner, the custodian smiled that big, toothy smile of hers. "Well, old Merle'll go with you, Sugar. I'll help you. I've done this plenty of times. No problem!"

So the three of us headed to my old brown sedan. A rookie teacher who wasn't a teacher at all, a small child who couldn't talk plainly, and a custodian who knew everything. I felt pretty comfortable with the situation.

"Where does, uh, he, live, Mr. Adams?" Miss Merle asked, nodding her head in the direction of the back seat where "Buddy" was sitting.

"Mrs. Foster said he lives in a duplex on Second Street. Any idea where that might be?"

"Sure I do, Mr. Adams. I'll get you over there. Sugar, I know every street in this town. Now turn left out of the parking lot and head towards town. It's not far." Merle smiled with an air of confidence as we rode along, and she chattered away about first one thing and then another. Without a break in her talking, she announced, "Turn right at the next street. That's Second Street. Those apartments are just as you make the turn."

I kept the old sedan at a snail's crawl as we rolled slowly by the row of apartments. Glancing in the rearview mirror, I noticed Buddy looking through the car window with a blank look on his face.

"Do you recognize your house, Buddy?" No answer. Finally, I pulled over to the curb and got out of the car. Opening the backdoor, I reached in and took the boy's hand. He slid out and stood beside me on the sidewalk. Miss Merle got out, too. The three of us started walking back down the street, pausing in front of each door. "Buddy" just looked at each apartment, and didn't react.

I was about to give up when Buddy started jumping up and down.

"Da by ous! Da by ous!" He ran up to the door with Miss Merle and me close on his heels. He was about to run in when I pulled him back.

"Wait, Buddy! Let's knock on the door and make sure we have the right place." The boy peered up at me with a puzzled look on his face, but held back. Taking charge, I firmly knocked on the door.

I glanced around at Miss Merle and smiled when we heard voices coming from inside the apartment. Turning back to face the door, I assumed my most professional manner by standing straight and casually resting my arm over "Buddy's" small shoulders. Then, the door opened. Wide.

Standing in the open doorway, naked as the day she was born, was a woman. Definitely a woman. A large, dark-skinned, naked woman!

I tried not to stare, but I couldn't help it! The woman was naked! Not a stitch! I couldn't say a word. I was speechless! I turned desperately back to Miss Merle for help, but that didn't work. She was staring, too, with her mouth wide open.

I turned back to the woman in the doorway. She was still naked! She made no attempt to cover herself at all! I cleared my throat and tried to look over her head, but I could still see an awful lot of bare body. A lot more than I wanted to see!

"Uh, I'm, uh, Johnny…uh, Mr. Johnny…uh…Mr. Adams Johnny…No, Johnny, uh, Adams." I looked way above her head, but I could still see the body parts.

The lady in the door put her hands on her ample, bare hips. "You Marcus's teacher from over at the school?"

I nodded my head up and down, trying to keep my eyes focused up high. The next thing I knew that naked lady was reaching out to shake my hand. Oh, Lawdy! I had to look down for the briefest moment, so I just squeezed my eyes shut while that woman shook my hand. I still saw too much!

"Thank you so much for bringing my boy here home, Mr.... did you say... Adams? I know I shoulda brought Marcus to school today, it being his first day and all, but I've been so busy! I'll come over as soon as I have time, though, and sign his papers and stuff. I know he don't talk so good, but he's a real smart boy."

Focusing back at the roofline of the apartment, I nodded my head again. I looked back at Merle, but she was still staring with her mouth gaped open even wider than before.

I didn't turn back around. I grabbed Merle's arm and led her to the car, mumbling something about us having to go. Keeping my eyes straight ahead, I somehow managed to drive the car down Second Street and back to the school. Inside the car was dead silence, all the way back.

I pulled up to the school and stopped the car to let Miss Merle out.

"I can't believe what we just saw," I said to the quiet custodian. "Can you?"

Not hearing a response, I looked over at Merle. She was staring straight ahead, with her mouth still drooping open. Without a word, she opened the car door and got out.

Somehow I managed to drive home, breaking, turning, and accelerating, and wondered how I'd ever face that woman when she came to fill out the boy's papers. I really shouldn't have worried, though, because when she came to the school, I passed right by her and didn't recognize her. She had on clothes!

TWENTY-ONE

IT TOOK ONLY THREE days of working with the speech therapist for us to figure out "Buddy's" real name. Marcus Jones. What had he called himself? Oh, yes...M'tus Doan. Now why hadn't I understood that! And...Mrs. Foster was right! Marcus was six years old. He had told us that. I remembered so clearly because I had repeated it over and over trying to make some sense out of it....'tic be'r doad.' I had to admit. 'Tic be'r doad' still didn't sound anything like 'six years old' to me!

So Marcus stayed in my class. That was a good thing, because everybody loved him. Especially Percival, who called him, 'Frenchie' for the rest of the year. He fit right in.

The days flew by at a rapid rate. Before I knew it, Friday had rolled around again. Another week of being a teacher. The children in my class pretty much settled into a routine and were, for the most part, patient with my continued struggles at trying to juggle all the things that go into teaching. I must have improved somewhat, because on occasion, I even got a high five or a nod and right-on pointed finger from good old Percival.

In a week's time, the days of winter disappeared and hints of spring appeared. The trees that had seemed dead and bare suddenly burst out in fluffy leaves and multi-colored blossoms. The grass that had been withered and brown for months took on a vibrant green. And best of all, the birds returned from wherever they had been, and their voices sang lilting melodies outside our classroom windows.

Inside the classroom, things were changing, too. Without realizing it, 'Techr's' class was fast becoming, my class. Everyday, the children were learning! I was amazed! I could actually see their reading improving each day! A light bulb even came on with Tremaine and Zach, who were in my lowest reading group. After working all week on the same words, those boys suddenly started recognizing how the letters fit together to make words. I was so excited that I promised I would play softball with them at recess.

After lunch we headed outside, in a line this time. Tremaine and Zach carried the bat and ball, chattering away to each other. By the time we reached the playing field, they had decided that I was going to be the catcher for both teams. The guys didn't want the girls to play, but I told them they had to include the girls. So, reluctantly, they chose teams, leaving the girls as last picks. I flipped a coin and the game began.

Of course, Percival was the pitcher for his team. He was pretty good for a tiny, little first grader. Most of the balls he threw came somewhere near home plate, although a few of them sailed over my head, and three hit me on the arm and leg. I didn't complain too much since the ball was old and very soft.

Mike, Raymond, and Randy struck at everything Percival threw. In a few short minutes, they all made outs. Then Percival's team came in to bat. I was surprised when Percival told the girls to bat first. Mary Anne just about knocked everybody down pushing her way up to the plate. Percival tried to show her how to hold the bat, but he got shoved away.

"I know how to bat, Mr. Smarty Pants!" Mary Anne glared at Percival. Percival darted back quickly, because nobody messed with Mary Anne. She was bigger than all of the boys, especially Percival, and bossy didn't even begin to describe her nature. True to her word, Mary Anne hit the ball. It blooped a few feet past the pitcher. All ten of the children on the other side ran after it. They fell in a heap when they reached the ball, scrambling and fighting for it. While all of this was going on, Mary Anne chug-a-lugged around the bases on her little chunky legs. She made a home run on a ball that went all of twenty feet!

I gave Mary Anne a high five when she crossed home plate. "Good job, Mary Anne!"

"Thank you, Mr. Adams," Mary Anne said with a big smile. Prissing over to sit down, she passed Percival and stuck her tongue out at him.

Sweet, little Jessica with the hazel eyes came up next to bat. When she got to the plate, she just stood there. Percival, who had assigned himself captain of the team, hollered, "Pick up the bat, Jessica!"

Looking back at Percival, Jessica dropped her head and blinked her long, thick eyelashes.

"I don't know how to hold it. Can you help me?"

Sighing loudly, as if he had the weight of the world on his scrawny little shoulders, Percival walked over to Jessica and picked up the bat.

"Okay. Put one hand here and the other one here." Percival pointed to the spots on the bat. Jessica shyly reached over and put her small hands on the bat.

"Is this right, Percival?" Jessica looked up with a slight smile on her face. I couldn't believe what I was seeing! That little first grade girl with the long dark lashes was flirting with Percival! She was good at it, too! Shy, quiet little Jessica! Poor old Percival didn't have a chance.

"Yeah, Jessica! Now hit the ball!" The ball came loping over the base, and Jessica swung the bat. She missed it about two feet.

"That's okay, Jessica. Try again! Hold the bat just like I showed you to do!"

"Like this, Percival?" Jessica put her hands about a foot apart on the bat. Percival walked back over and pulled her right hand down.

"That's the way it should be, Jessica. Now hit the next one!" Malcolm with the missing front teeth threw the ball.

Jessica swung, but too late. The ball dropped in the dirt behind her.

"You have one more strike, Jessica. Try to remember what I told you to do and keep your eyes on the ball this time!" Percival yelled.

Jessica looked back under those thick, black lashes and smiled at Percival. "Okay, Percival. I'll try to remember." Malcolm threw the ball. Whack! Jessica swung the bat like a pro and connected! The ball went sailing over Malcolm's head and landed outfield. Jessica started running! In no time flat, she had rounded all the bases and ran across home plate.

The team cheered and ran toward her. All but Percival. He just crossed his arms over his bony chest, tapped his foot in the dirt, and smirked.

Handing the bat to Porsha, he announced, loudly, "Now, Porsha, see what you can do when you listen to me? Hold the bat this way and do what Jessica did!" Percival demonstrated the holding of the bat again.

Porsha hit the first ball that was pitched to her. She ran to first base. Madalyn came up to bat next. After missing the first two balls by a mile, she whacked the third one past the first baseman. She all but danced into first while Porsha made it to second. Tall, lanky Bonni also got a hit and loaded the bases.

Percival looked around. All of the girls on his team had batted. Glancing over at the boys all clamoring up to bat, Percival announced that he would be the next batter.

"Hey, back off! We need a hit to bring all those girls in! Now get back! I'm going to smack that old ball all the way to the fence."

I'm not exactly sure what happened next. I saw Malcolm throw the ball, and the next thing I remember was waking up in the hospital with a concussion! The best that I can piece together from all of the children's stories is that Percival did smack the ball all the way to the fence. But in the process of trying to be a hero, he let the bat fly out of his hands, and it whacked me right in the head!

It took me all weekend to recuperate, and by Monday morning I still had a slight headache and a whopper of a black eye. Even so, I felt like I could make it back to school. I was standing at the doorway to my class when the children arrived.

"Hey, Techr! Yo' eye's black!"

"Mr. Adams? You got a black eye!"

"Techr, you know you got a black eye?"

Percival finally walked into the room, cutting his eyes up at me. He didn't say anything as he walked quietly to his desk in the back of the room.

"Good morning, Percival," I called back to him. "Are you going to be able to help me today? I want to rearrange the desks."

Percival looked up at me with a lopsided smile. "Yeah, I can, Techr. You gonna need some help with that shiner you got!"

Smiling, I walked over to my desk and started to call the roll. My eye hurt like the dickens, but I didn't let on. I knew I had to be tough for Percival. Another week of being a teacher had begun, and I knew right then and there that being a teacher sometimes hurt!

TWENTY-TWO

I WAS BUSILY preparing for Tuesday when Mrs. Foster came over the intercom to remind all teachers about the faculty meeting in the school library. Hurriedly, I gathered up the materials I needed to take home and headed down the hall.

As luck would have it, I was the last one to enter the room. I looked around for a seat while a deathly quiet settled in among the teachers. Everyone stared at me as if I was a freak or something! Suddenly I remembered my eye. I looked from side to side, trying to include each person. Then I shrugged my shoulders and pointed to the eye that was black.

"Percival."

Laughter erupted immediately, and the usual teacher chatter resumed. I continued to search for a seat, when I spotted Anastasia sitting off by herself at the back table. She motioned for me to come and sit at the table with her. I quickly walked over and put my things down. That's when I got a good look at the chair where I was to sit. It was all of eight inches from the floor and about that same width. It was just about the right size for tiny, little Percival!

Anastasia laughed, "Just ease yourself down and hope you hit the chair. With time, you won't even think these little bitty chairs are strange at all!"

I looked down at my long legs. Very slowly I lowered my long body until I finally made contact with the very small seat of the miniature chair. My legs were sprawled out across the floor, and my behind was hanging off a good four inches on each side. Anastasia put her hand over her mouth, but I could tell by the merry twinkle in her big brown eyes and the frequent bumping of her shoulders that she was having a good laugh. I think I even heard a snort, but I'm not sure.

Suddenly everybody in the room was laughing, even the principal. I really didn't see anything that was so funny. I decided right then and there that teachers were a strange lot. And here I was...one of them!

Most of the meeting was about standards, whatever that was, and the upcoming testing program. I sensed some tense moments when the principal stated over and over that the test scores had to increase.

At the end of the meeting, Mrs. Foster announced that a new family from Russia was moving into our area. She said they had a seven year old boy who would be entering our first grade. Then she looked at me.

"Mr. Adams, this little boy has been without a father for quite some time, and I believe he needs a father figure in his young life. I'm planning to put him in your class since you are the only male teacher in the first grade. I feel like you will be good with him."

At that precise moment, my eight inch chair that I had tottering on two legs slipped out from under me, and I sprawled out awkwardly on the library floor. As the laughter became hysterical in the room, I propped up on one arm and looked up at the principal.

"Well, Mrs. Foster, I'll do my best to be a good role model for the little Russian boy."

Amidst unladylike fits of laughing from everyone in the room, including the principal, the meeting ended. I waited on the floor for the faulty members to exit the room before I got up and left.

As I walked to my car, several of the teachers passed by, patted me on the back, and continued to giggle. I flopped down in my old car and got really mad. I was so mad I forgot to push in the clutch to start the car, and it jumped and sputtered to an abrupt halt. I slowly peered over the steering wheel to see if anyone was watching. Of course they were! Still laughing, too. Crouching low, I gave a jaunty salute to my merry audience and drove home. I had a black eye, a sore seat from the fall in the teeny little chair, a boy from Russia entering my class tomorrow, and my fellow co-workers laughing their heads off at me.

And it was only Monday!

TWENTY-THREE

THE NEXT MORNING I was standing outside my classroom bright and early, smiling at the children and exchanging friendly greetings with the teachers who passed by me, when the new student from Russia arrived. Mrs. Foster introduced the boy as Iouli Chekhov. I couldn't help but stare!

The boy was nothing short of beautiful! He had a Slavic look, with light brown hair and green eyes. His sparkling white teeth were perfectly aligned, and his skin was quite fair and flawless. He was tall for a first grader and dressed quite fashionably in a blue wind suit.

"Hello, Iouli. I'm Mr. Adams, your teacher." The boy looked down and shuffled his pointed-toed feet nervously. The boy's mother quickly spoke something in Russian as she nudged her son forward. Without taking his eyes from the floor, Iouli stuck out his small hand and said something that I sure didn't understand. Russian!

"Iouli doesn't speak English yet, Mr. Adams," the

principal interjected. "But, we'll get him some extra help and have him fluent in no time!"

My mind was whirling as I pondered the situation. I was not a trained teacher. I was struggling, myself, just to get through each day, and now I had a student who couldn't speak English. A scared-to-death little fellow from another country who was under my care to guide and teach him. How did I manage to get myself into such messes!

Taking a big gulp of air and praying silently, I grabbed the boy's hand and enwrapped it in my own. "Come on in, Iouli. Let me introduce you to the other children and find you a desk." Iouli walked along beside me, and we entered the room.

"Boys and girls. We have a new student in our class. His name is Iouli, and he is from Russia. He doesn't speak much English, so we'll all have to help him understand what we're saying and doing."

"Does he speak French like Marcus?" I looked back at good old Percival and shook my head.

"No, Percival. Iouli speaks Russian, because he is from Russia."

"How come he don't speak French? Ain't Russia in France since it ain't in this country?"

I scratched my head at Percival's logic. "Russia is a different country from France and the United States where we live. People from different countries speak different languages. You understand that, Percival? What about it, Class? You understand?"

"Nope." Percival quickly turned his attention to Iouli,

who had a blank look on his face, obviously not comprehending anything that we were saying.

"Say something." When Iouli didn't respond, Percival got right in his face and spoke louder. "I said, say something!"

Iouli looked at me for help, but I knew I couldn't speak Russian. Then I thought...hand gestures. So I pointed to Iouli's lips and wiggled my fingers. Then I pointed my finger at him.

Iouli shook his head and smiled timidly. "Iouli." I about jumped for joy. He understood. Then I pointed to myself.

"I am Mr. Adams," I said rather loudly and very slowly. I then pointed to Percival. "He is Percival. Per-ci-val."

"Per-ci-val," Iouli said with a big smile on his face. Percival grinned from ear to ear. He threw his freckled arm around Iouli's waist and led him to a seat in the back of the room. Percival pointed to the desk.

"Desk," he told Iouli. Pointing to Iouli he replied, "Your desk."

"Desk, your desk," Iouli said as he sat down in the desk.

Percival looked back at me and hunched his shoulders. "Don't worry, Techr. I'll take care o' this boy. I'll have 'em speaking right in no time. Jes' leave it to me. And ya' wrong, Techr. That boy sure 'nuff is speakin' French. I know French when I hear it!"

Once again I let Percival take over a difficult situation. I knew it would not be good for Iouli to learn English from Percival, but it took the monkey off my back. Besides,

Iouli seemed to like Percival right off, so I figured he'd be okay. He'd just be a Russian speaking slangy English, that's all.

And I was right! Before the day was over, I heard Iouli, the little Russian boy, who, according to Percival, spoke French, say ain't and nuttin'. But he was happy, and that was what mattered. And what a pair they made…big, tall Iouli and short, tiny Percival. They became great friends!

I breathed a sigh of relief when the final bell rang for dismissal that day. Actually, as far as my days as a teacher had gone, it had been an okay day. I smiled and felt rather good when my class of now twenty-two students left the room to go home.

You just might make it, Old Buddy, I thought to myself. *You just might make it!*

TWENTY-FOUR

IT TOOK NO TIME for Iouli to master the English language, and his accent became less pronounced with everyday that passed. He and Percival were inseparable friends. Everywhere you saw one, you saw the other. If the truth be known, all the kids loved Iouli. He was just that kind of fellow.

Another Friday rolled around before I knew it. I had always heard that time flies when you're having fun, and I have to admit that 'Techr's' class of first graders was growing on me. I felt important in the lives of these little people, and it was a good feeling.

The only black spot in my weekend was a call from my dad. I made some promises to him that I'd return to school soon, but they were weak promises, mainly to get him off the phone so that I could plan my instruction for the next week. He finally hung up, and I was able to get back to what was really important to me at the time. Getting ready for Monday!

I arrived at school early on Monday and quickly went outside the end door to do my first official stint on bus duty. I looked around to see who was on bus duty with me, but about that time the first bus arrived, so I never saw who came to help.

It was a beautiful, clear day, and everything went fine for the first five minutes. Then I noticed a group of boys gathered at the end of the building. I walked casually over to see what they were doing.

"Good morning, guys. Why are you all over here instead of in the cafeteria?" I leaned my head into the group and had a double take! Two of the boys were holding open a magazine...apparently the centerfold of the magazine. Lined up on the two pages were pictures of naked men, standing in a row. Tall, short, fat, thin...all shapes and sizes... naked men! It took me a few seconds to find my voice.

"Boys, who brought this magazine to school?"

The book suddenly went sailing down in the grass, and the ten or so boys ran inside the door and quickly found seats in the cafeteria. I reached down to pick up the magazine when another hand snatched it from me. I looked around. Rolling my eyes Heavenward, I stammered, "Good morning, Miss Picklesimmer."

By that time, the old sourpuss had opened the magazine, and her mouth was literally touching her chin, it was gaping open so widely. After a few moments of dead silence, the expected tongue-lashing began in earnest.

"Mr. Adams! I cannot believe this! This is filthy,

vulgar, nasty! I am taking it straight to the principal! I cannot believe you have this piece of trash at school!" With that, she stormed off to the principal's office.

Suddenly my beautiful Monday became gray and stormy…at least in my mind. I somehow managed to finish my time on bus duty and trudged slowly down to my classroom. Standing at the door was the principal, holding the offensive magazine in her hand. She was not smiling.

"Mr. Adams, I have put an assistant in your class for a while. Can you come to the office for a few minutes?"

Nodding my head, I slowly followed Mrs. Foster to her office. She closed the door behind me, then turned and handed me the magazine.

"Is this yours, Mr. Adams?"

I couldn't believe she was asking me that! "No!" I said emphatically. "No! I took it from some of the boys as they got off the bus this morning!"

Mrs. Foster doubled over laughing. When she finally regained her composure, I was just staring at her. I guess I had missed the joke.

Drying her eyes from the tears of uncontrollable laughter, the principal reached over and put her arm around my shoulders.

"Johnny, I knew this didn't belong to you. But I had to ask. Besides, Miss Picklesimmer was watching me like a hawk when I went to your room to get you. I had to play the part of the stern principal."

Mrs. Foster went into another fit of laughing. I just stared at her. I couldn't see what was so funny. Between guffaws, she said, "Oh, Johnny! If you had only been here when she brought in the magazine. She plopped it open on my desk and pointed to the row of men on the pages. Her index finger was right on, uh, one of the men's private parts. When she looked down and saw where she was pointing, she jerked her hand back as if it had been scorched or something! It was just so funny, but I couldn't laugh in front of her. I'm sorry! I just can't help it!"

Another fit of laughing resumed while I stood awkwardly watching the principal of the school totally lose it. Also, the offending magazine was open to that awful center page, and it made me want to cross my hands in front of myself.

For the life of me, I couldn't laugh with the principal. I was just too embarrassed, having that unclad line-up of men gawking up at me. After what seemed like an eternity, Mrs. Foster gained control of herself, picked up the magazine and handed it to me.

"Here, Johnny. Do something with this thing."

I quickly put my hands behind me and backed away, shaking my head from side to side.

"No way under God's green Earth will I touch that thing, Mrs. Foster. Uh-uh, no way! That's just not my kind of thing, and, personally, I don't want to ever see it again." With that said, I went back to my class.

I never did see that terrible magazine again. Mrs. Foster said she left it on her desk, with plans to destroy it after school. She never got the chance, because it mysteriously disappeared before the end of the day. I guess it must have been interesting to somebody for it to take missing so fast. I suspected the school secretary, because she had to have heard all that was said in the principal's office. Or it could have been Miss Merle, although I really didn't think that Bible quoting lady would have any use for it in the least. All I can say is that line-up of naked men went home with somebody that Monday in March!

Later that afternoon when I was working in my room, I looked on the calendar to see when my next day of bus duty would roll around. In two short weeks! I already dreaded it!

TWENTY-FIVE

TUESDAY WAS A pretty good day even though I got some weird looks from some of the teachers, especially Miss Picklesimmer. That is until lunch time rolled around.

I followed my class to the lunch room, and all the kids got their lunch plates without any mishaps. They were sitting quietly, eating their cheeseburgers and fries, when I came and sat between Dexter and Raymond.

I felt rather proud when I looked at my plate. It was heaped with fries and had a really big piece of chocolate cake next to the burger… an end piece with thick icing. Um-m…I couldn't wait to dig into that.

For one of the quietest boys in my class, Dexter was smacking away on his lunch. He had piled his steamy cheeseburger full of mustard and ketchup, and it dripped all over the place while he gulped that burger down in what must have been record speed. Raymond, on the other side of me, was trying to bribe Madalyn into giving him her burger.

I smiled as I listened to the smacking on one side of me and the expert political maneuvers on the other side. Just as I was about to take the first bite of my burger, Dexter scraped his plate clean and reached for his carton of chocolate milk. Temporarily forgetting that he had already opened his carton, he proceeded to shake the milk vigorously. A huge stream of chocolate milk came flying out of the carton, went up in a spiral, and landed directly on top of my head.

I just sat there, stunned, as the milk trickled down my face, over my shoulders, and onto my neatly creased, khaki pants. When I was able to open my eyes, I looked around at Dexter. He was sitting there staring at me with his mouth wide open. He was stark white, and the fear of the Lord was definitely on his face.

I stuck my tongue out and started licking the milk from around my mouth.

"Too bad you decided to give me your chocolate milk, Dexter. You really don't know what you're missing." Then I began to laugh. When the other children started laughing, too, Dexter finally took a breath.

"I'm sorry, Mr. Adams. I guess I forgot I'd already opened that carton o'milk," Dexter said in a small voice.

I reached over and put my milk soaked arm around Dexter's shoulders. "That's all right, Buddy. Accidents happen. Don't worry about it. Besides, I didn't like this old shirt anyway. Now I can get rid of it with no regrets."

Dexter grinned and breathed in another big gulp of air. He then leaned over and whispered in my ear. "You gonna tell my mama what I did? Cause she'll whup me for sure if she finds out."

"Shoot, no, Son. You didn't mean to soak me with your milk. It was an accident, pure and simple. Nothing your mama needs to know about. Now, why don't you go and get you another carton of milk."

"Thanks, Mr. Adams," Dexter whispered as he headed for the milk cooler.

All of a sudden a wad of paper towels scrunched across my face. I looked through them to see who was rubbing at my skin so hard. Percival! I should have known.

My aggravated look at Percival didn't deter him in the least.

"Now, Techr, hold still and let me get some o' that milk off yo' face. Jest look at you. You done gone and got yo'self in a mess!"

Percival was right. I was a mess. Mrs. Foster let me go home to shower and change clothes right after lunch. When I returned my class was working busily in their math workbooks.

I nodded for Patti, my teacher's assistant, to leave, and then just stood there and watched my twenty-two little first graders busy at work. They had ridiculed me, given me a black eye, soaked me in chocolate milk, broken my heart, and hugged my long legs more times than I could count. I sure was proud of that little class.

TWENTY-SIX

THE NEXT DAY I was teaching away at the front of the room when I heard someone calling me. At first I tried to ignore the voice saying over and over, "Techr. Techr. Techr." I finally paused in what was one of my finest lessons on community helpers. I was really into that lesson, too! It was about firemen, something I'd wanted to be since I was in the first grade.

I looked around the tousled heads in the row to see who was calling me. It was Beth, the short, little blonde with the soft-spoken voice.

"What is it, Beth? This better be important since you're interrupting my teaching you about all the things that firemen do for us."

Beth looked back at me with her big blue eyes and nodded her head up and down. "I b'lieve it's important, Techr." Then she said nothing. The room got very quiet, and it was then that I heard a thumping and moaning noise.

"Who's making that noise?" I asked in my best teacher

voice. "What is that strange noise?"

"That's why I was calling you, Techr. It's Martha Dee, and she's back here having a fit. Ya' need to come back here and see her." I frowned at Beth as I casually walked down the aisle to where she was sitting in the back of the room.

My eyes widened in horror as I looked at the spectacle on the floor. Sure enough, there was Martha Dee writhing and twisting in convulsions. She was foaming at the mouth, and her legs were jerking back and forth.

I yelled at the top of my voice. "Somebody get help! Something's wrong with Martha Dee! No! I'll get help! Just watch her!" I screamed as I ran from the room, leaving my entire class of first graders looking stunned, and one of their group on the floor, doing something really strange.

Breathless, I ran all the way down the hall, turned the corner, and continued my marathon run into the office at the end of the second hall.

"Somebody come… and… help me!" I gasped for breath looking wildly at the secretary. "It's one….it's Martha Dee…she's…on…the…floor!"

Mrs. Foster came flying out of her office and ran back with me to my room. She rushed to Martha Dee's side, knelt down,and cradled the child's head on her lap.

"It's okay, Martha Dee. It's okay," the principal said calmly to the shaking child. "Someone please hand me a wet paper towel."

Cameron, the boy closest to the sink, jumped up from his desk and grabbed a handful of towels. He soaked them to the point of dripping and hurried back to hand them to the principal.

"Thank you, Son." Mrs. Foster wiped Martha Dee's forehead, all the while, talking to her in soft, soothing tones. I stood by like a three-footed klutz, wringing my hands, praying profusely, and watching the principal work her magic.

Looking over her shoulder, Mrs. Foster nodded for me to lean down. "You might want to take the other children outside for a few minutes, Mr. Adams."

"You don't need my help with Martha Dee, Mrs. Foster?" Immediately I knew that was a dumb question! The principal looked back at me with one eyebrow up. I recognized immediate displeasure on her face.

"No, Mr. Adams. You take care of the other children, and I'll try to manage Martha Dee without you."

Later that day as I reflected back to the emergency with Martha Dee, I realized that the principal had cut me down, badly! Not that I didn't deserve it, but she had cut me down.

Not only that, but it seemed that the entire school knew that Martha Dee had seizures occasionally, and no one had remembered to tell me about it. The joke around the school for the next couple of days was that the medical student, turned teacher, went berserk when Martha Dee had a seizure. I even heard that Miss "Sourpuss" said she didn't want me to ever doctor on her! I wished fervently that I was a doctor when I heard that! I would have taken that old biddy and sewn her mouth up tight as a drum!

I learned a valuable lesson from Martha Dee's experience. It's not very smart for a teacher to leave an entire class, especially first graders, by themselves while another student is in the floor, maybe dying. But I did, and I couldn't change what I did, so I moved on…with a red face…and a tag of humiliation trailing behind me…but I moved on…to another day that hopefully would be a little easier to handle.

TWENTY-SEVEN

MARTHA DEE CAME back to school the next day looking fit as a fiddle. The children treated her the same as always. As for me, I watched her like a hawk throughout the morning. I think Martha Dee enjoyed the attention I was giving her, because she kept looking at me and smiling, but I had to be prepared when and if she had another seizure in my class.

I had studied my medical books with a passion the night before at 'Techr's' house and knew every procedure to follow when someone had a seizure. One thing I knew for sure…not to run down the hall screaming for help.

It was Friday, and everything went well throughout the entire morning. With Martha Dee looking robust and healthy, I finally settled down and taught with a fervor, expecting all of my students to become Junior Einsteins by lunchtime.

Not wanting to waste a single minute of learning time, I called the last reading group to the reading circle shortly before lunch. I noticed that Brennan and Luke dragged a little as they approached the circle, but I attributed their lack of enthusiasm to the fact that it was almost lunchtime, and they were getting hungry.

"Hurry, guys," I prodded. "We don't have much time." The boys sat down in the tiny little chairs, holding their books on their laps. They both stared at the floor.

"What's the matter, fellows? You hungry?" Luke looked up at me with his blue eyes drooping. Just as he started to answer me, his face turned white as a ghost. He put his little hand over his mouth and tried to stop the vomit that came spewing out between his fingers. The other children in the circle jumped up and screamed as vomit went everywhere! It covered Luke's reading book, his shirt, his pants, and his chair. It splattered on the floor, the other chairs, and my shoes.

Trying to remain calm, I stood up and motioned for the other children to move to the side of the room. Stepping over the muddled-up, smelly mess of scrambled eggs, bacon bits, and chocolate milk, apparently Luke's breakfast, I put my hand on Luke's trembling, bony shoulders and led him to the restroom. After cleaning the sick boy as best as I could with paper towels, I walked over to the door with my arm still around him.

"Percival. Could you please go to the health room and get the school nurse to come down here?" Percival headed out the door, then turned back.

"I'll get Miss Merle, too, Techr. She'll clean up that mess Luke's done made on the floor."

"Thank you, Percival. I was planning on telling you to get Miss Merle, too."

Percival frowned at me as he headed out the door. I heard him as he went down the hall. "Sure he wuz…sure he wuz. Pore ole Techr. He still don't know too much."

I took the rest of the class down to the main restrooms to wash their hands for lunch, trying to put out of my mind the remarks that Percival had made. Making an attempt to act very official and teacher-like, I lined the children up outside my classroom and waited for Percival to return. I had Luke stand on the other side of the hall, since he had a strong smell of throw-up on him. His face was still very pale, and all of my doctor instincts told me that he had a stomach virus. Miss Merle came by with a bucket and mop, scowling at me as if it was my fault that Luke had thrown up in the classroom. After cleaning up the smelly mess, she left with a loud, disgusted sigh.

Percival finally returned with the nurse in tow. She took one look at Luke and carted him off to the health room.

"I'll call his mother to come and get him," the nurse said over her shoulder as she went down the hall.

"Okay. Now, boys and girls, let's go to lunch!"

Well, that turned into a total fiasco! As we walked down the hall, Brennan started throwing up. He splattered the floors and the walls and some of the children. He began to cry, and the other children started hollering and shrieking trying to escape yet another round of smelly vomit coming their way.

Without being told, Percival headed back to the office in search of the nurse and Miss Merle. I got the class somewhat under control and away from that round of vomit, when Josh joined the throw-up group. Now I don't know to this day what that boy had for breakfast, but it had to be something strange, because it stunk to high heaven!

I herded the remaining children out of the way just as Miss Merle appeared with her bucket and mop again. Giving me a killer look, she preceded to clean up the two new vomit piles. When she finished, she looked at Brennan and Josh, standing over to one side, covered in vomit.

"Come on here, boys. Miss Merle'll take you to the nurse. Come on now. Miss Merle'll take care o'you." The two sick boys rushed into the ample arms of the custodian and headed for the health room. I took the remaining children back to the restroom to clean up. Then we headed down to the lunch room.

The last child had just gotten her plate and sat down when I came to the table. I looked at my plate. It was piled high with hash and rice. Normally, I love hash and rice. And Mrs. Boyd had really piled it on. But something about it didn't appeal to me. The longer I looked at it, the sicker I felt.

I looked around at the children in my class, and they were all staring at that hash just like I was doing. What happened next, I can't really recall. I'm not exactly sure who was first, but everybody in my little class started throwing up, including me. Vomit went everywhere! Some children were crying, some wet their pants, and the other children in the cafeteria went running out, knocking each other down in their pandemonium. I guess all of the children got home that afternoon. All I really remember is the nurse telling me to go on home and take care of myself, and Miss Merle going back down the hall with her mop and bucket. I threw up twice on my way to 'Techr's' house and more times than I could count through the course of the weekend.

By Monday morning, my virus was gone; my weekend was gone; my lesson plans for the upcoming week were not done; and I was weak as a newborn puppy. But I went to school. I had to go. It just didn't seem right for the teacher who was filling in for the missing teacher to call in sick!

TWENTY-EIGHT

MONDAY ACTUALLY turned out to be an uneventful day. Six of the children were still out with the virus bug, and the rest of the class was quiet and listless all day long. They mostly kept their heads down throughout the day, and spoke softly or not at all.

I tried to teach some, but not feeling too well myself, we resorted to a lot of ETV for the better part of the day. I noticed at lunch that no one seemed to have much of an appetite, and the children even asked me after lunch if they could stay inside for recess. That suited me fine, since I still felt like a vacuum cleaner had sucked out my insides.

When the final bell rang for dismissal at the end of the day, my little first graders left the room as quietly as they had entered that morning. I left right behind them, drove slowly home, and piled under 'Techr's' handmade afghan on the old blue couch and slept the afternoon away. I woke up at six o'clock the next morning, hungry as a bear and anxious to get to school. I had survived the virus and was ready to take on the world inside my little first grade classroom!

A rambunctious group of first graders entered my room that Tuesday morning…all twenty-two of them! The virus bug had definitely moved on to other places and people and left in its wake a lot of built up energy waiting to be unleashed.

The kids compared colors of puke for the first ten minutes of the day until I finally put a stop to it. Percival even suggested that we all draw and color pictures of our own vomit and vote on who had the best picture! I vetoed that suggestion, too. Much to the chagrin of the children, we finally settled into our usual routine of early morning reading groups, and the morning whipped by at an alarming rate of speed.

Bonni finished her workbook page in a hurry as usual and asked me to color a page in her Cinderella coloring book. I told her I'd do it some other time since I was busy helping some of the other children with their workbook pages. She hung her little head and walked quietly back to her desk.

Later that morning we worked on math. I actually think I did a pretty good job of teaching the "Fact Families;" at least I felt good about it. The children were all working quietly at their seats when I felt a tug on my sleeve. I looked around, and there stood Bonni again.

"Mr. Techr. I already finished my adding. Can you color my picture of Cinderella now?"

"I'm sorry, Bonni. It's almost time to go to lunch. Why

don't you go color in your book until we wash hands for lunch?" I turned from the disappointed child as I made a final loop through the lines of desks to make sure all of the children were on track with the math. I didn't see Bonni's sad eyes following me.

After lunch I took the children out to recess. I didn't notice that Bonni had taken her Cinderella coloring book and crayons outside until I'd walked over to stand beside Miss Briggs with the big brown eyes.

"Did the bad old virus get your class, too?" I asked the pretty first grade teacher.

"Yes, but from what I hear, your class got hit the hardest! I guess you know that you're the talk of the school again!"

This time I laughed with Anastasia. I guess we had made the top of the gossip chain in the school with our flood of vomit in the cafeteria.

"I've never been so sick in all my life! I thought I would throw up my toe nails!" Anastasia laughed that contagious laugh of hers when I felt someone tapping me on the leg. I looked down, and there stood Bonni, poking that infernal Cinderella coloring book at me again.

"Can ya' color a page now, Mr. Techr? I been saving a special one for you to color." The skinny little girl had her pixie face turned up to me.

"Bonni, Honey, this is not a good time for me to color in your book. Besides, you should run and play with the other children. You need to get some exercise. Run on now, while I talk to Miss Briggs a minute."

Bonni's eyes drooped as she sauntered off, clutching that precious coloring book tightly in her little hand. I watched her and sighed deeply.

"That child is about to drive me crazy to color in her coloring book. I wish she'd drop it. I'd feel pretty stupid coloring Cinderella at this stage of my life!"

Anastasia laughed again, and we chatted easily for the next few minutes before we both had to gather up our little charges and head back into the school building.

I didn't really keep count, but I believe Bonni had to ask me at least fifty times through the rest of that week to color Cinderella in her coloring book. And...I turned her down each time with some excuse or other.

By Friday afternoon, I had run out of excuses, and I was really exasperated with her begging me every few minutes to color a picture of Cinderella. When she asked me for the umpteenth time to color in her coloring book, I grabbed the thing out of her hand.

"Okay, Bonni! Give me that book!" Bonni smiled a huge grin from ear to ear as she handed me her prized Cinderella coloring book. I sat down at my desk and started coloring away.

That was probably the first time I had colored in a coloring book in fifteen years. I started with Cinderella's dress. I colored it pink and blue. It started to look pretty good so I added some touches of yellow to the bows on the sleeves. That really looked good.

Several children came up to my desk to ask me questions about their writing assignment, but I sent them away to do it by themselves, because I was really getting into the Cinderella coloring thing. I colored all of the birds that were tying the sash on Cinderella's dress a pretty shade of blue. Now, that really looked good.

I was thinking that I surely hadn't lost my knack for coloring when I sensed someone standing by my desk, watching me. Assuming it was one of the children again, and without looking up, I put out my hand to shoo whoever it was away.

"Go sit down and finish your work. Can't you see I'm busy?"

A low male voice answered me. "Yes, I can certainly see that you are busy all right! And I wouldn't disturb you for anything!"

I slowly eased my eyes upward and gazed into the eyes of the school district superintendent! My heart sank to my feet! The superintendent! The first time he had ever been in my classroom, and I was sitting at my desk, coloring Cinderella! I just about died on the spot! I put my head down into my hands in humiliation.

When I had the courage to look up again, my important visitor was gone. I saw him from time to time after that day, and he never mentioned the coloring book incident. Nor did I. I figured that some things are just better left unsaid. Especially anything related to Cinderella!

TWENTY-NINE

AS MARCH ROLLED INTO APRIL, my dad called a lot, checking to see if I was still at 'Techr's' house, I guess. And…he also knew that my finals were close at hand.

At that point in my life I really didn't want to be pressured by my dad…about staying at 'Techr's' house or about med school. So I had caller ID put on 'Techr's' phone, and every time Dad's number flashed up, I let the answering machine pick up with 'Techr's' voice on the message. The guys back at the university were only too happy to cover for me since I had their use of my snazzy car hanging over their heads. So as far as I knew, my dad assumed I was still at the university, plugging away on my med courses.

My dad really wasn't at the top of my priority list at that time. The circus was! All of the first grade teachers were taking their classes, as a group, on a field trip to the circus. And…since I was, in essence, a first grade teacher, I was expected to take my class along with the others.

I was excited and full of anxiety at the same time! I was excited because I hadn't been to a circus since I was a little boy...and...the brown-eyed Miss Briggs had said that my class could ride on the same bus as hers.

The anxiety jumped in when I thought about trying to manage my twenty-two first graders at a circus. And...then there was Miss Picklesimmer! She still didn't like me, and the thought of her watching my every move for an entire day about unraveled me.

Of course Percival heard about the first grade trip before I made up my mind to take my class along. He heard some of the children from the other classes talking about it at recess one day, and believe me, he didn't let it rest.

"We goin' to the circus with the other first grades, Techr? That big ole boy in Miss Davis' class told me they wuz' goin'." Percival followed me in from recess, pounding me with questions.

"I haven't decided yet, Percival. Now go take your seat so we can get started with our health lesson."

"But I wanna know if we're goin' to the circus with those other kids. How come you ain't decided yet?" Percival was relentless with his questions.

"I just haven't decided yet, Percival. Now go and sit down in your desk."

"But doncha' think ya' ought to take us to the circus with the other first grades? Look at all those kids out there, Techr. I bet haff of'em ain't never been to the circus. I think ya' outta take us, since so many ain't never been."

My patience was really wearing thin. "Percival! Go to

your desk and sit down! I told you I haven't decided yet about the circus!"

Percival dropped his head and looked under his eyebrows with a scowl as he scuffled back to his seat. "I wish our real 'Techr' wuz back! She'd take us to the circus and not have to think about it! I wish she wuz still here!"

That did it! I walked back to Percival's desk and looked down at him.

"All right, Percival! All right! I'll take you to the circus!"

Every child in the class jumped up from their desks and started cheering and talking and laughing…all at the same time. I stood by Percival's desk and watched the pandemonium in the room. At that precise moment, my anxiety level hit a record high! I had just told twenty-two first graders that I would take them on a bus to another town, fifty miles away, for the entire day, to go to the circus! I had to be crazy!

After school that day, I hurried to find Anastasia. She was in her portable classroom, straightening the students' desks. I knocked gently on the door as I crouched my long, lanky frame in order to watch my cohort through the small window above the doorknob.

Anastasia turned quickly around to look at the door causing her dark brown ponytail to whip across her pretty face.

"Well, look who's visiting the outer realm this afternoon. What a treat to have someone visit my far out classroom! Come on in, Johnny. Did you get lost?"

"Well, frankly, Miss Briggs, I came to get some help. I told my class that I would take them to the circus with you guys, but now I don't have a clue as to what I need to do next. Can you help me?"

"Anastasia."

I frowned at the young teacher standing before me.

"What?"

"Call me Anastasia."

"Uh, okay…Anastasia. Can you help me?"

Anastasia laughed. "You sure you don't want to get help from Miss Picklesimmer?"

Relaxing a little, I rolled my eyes back in my head. "No way! I don't want anything to do with the 'Wicked Witch of the West!' You're actually the only one I trust in our grade level."

"Well, I'll take that as a compliment, Mr. Adams!"

"Johnny."

Anastasia threw her head back and laughed. "Yes, right! Johnny. Okay, Johnny, let's get you ready to go to the circus!"

I moaned when Anastasia gave me the list of all the things I had to do to prepare for the big day. A letter home to the parents. Parent permission forms. Money collection forms, parent chaperones, and the list went on and on. The clincher was that I had to get all of it out by the next day since the trip was in two weeks.

With only grabbing a couple of hours sleep, I had every form, letter, phone number, and regulation completed by six o'clock the next morning. I prepared each child a packet to take home and told them that the packets had to be back to me by the next day if they wanted to go to the circus.

Surprisingly enough, all twenty-two children brought in their forms the next morning with only two or three suspicious-looking signatures among the lot. Well…I figured some of the parents really couldn't spell their own names correctly…or write in cursive. I had signatures and that was good enough for me! Three parents volunteered to chaperone my class, so in one day flat my first graders were all set to go to the circus! Only nine days to wait!

THIRTY

BY THE END OF THE next two weeks leading up to the trip to the circus, I was totally exhausted. The children were so excited they couldn't sit still; they didn't listen; and they must have asked me four thousand times when we were going to the circus. I found out pretty quick that first graders have no concept of time, days, or weeks.

The big day finally arrived on a cool, blustery day in April. I went to school very early that Friday morning so I'd be ready to load my twenty-two students on the bus with Anastasia's group as soon as the buses arrived.

By seven-thirty that morning, my three chaperones and all of my students had shown up except for Percival. I was more than a little puzzled by Percival's absence since he always rode the bus to school and therefore arrived early each day.

My eyes darted to the door frequently while I gave out name tags, went over the rules for the trip one last time, and sent each child to the restroom to at least try to use it before we got on the bus. Still, Percival did not show up.

I was really worried when Mrs. Foster announced over the speaker that our buses were lined up outside the cafeteria, and we should begin loading. I quickly sent a note to Sheila in the office to call Percival's house to see what was wrong. The dedicated secretary came running back to my room a few moments later and said she'd received no answer at Percival's house.

Reluctantly, I lined the other students up and led them to the waiting bus. Anastasia was standing at the door of the bus with her arms folded across her chest.

"What took you so long, Mr. Adams? I've had to do some tall talking to keep another class from taking your seats."

Watching my little group run to their seats on the big bus, I counted again, knowing I'd only come up with twenty-one again.

"Percival didn't show up this morning. I don't know what's wrong. He never misses, and he was so excited about this trip. I just know something's happened!"

Anastasia laid her hand gently on my arm, and ordinarily, that would have excited the heck out of me, but all I could feel at that moment was a great big lump in my throat and panic beyond belief consuming my entire body.

Mrs. Foster stuck her head in the door of the bus.

"Do you have everybody?"

"Yes, Ma'am, all of my students are here," Anastasia answered quietly. "But Mr. Adams is missing one who was supposed to go."

"Who's not here, Mr. Adams?"

I sighed heavily. "Percival."

"Oh, I'm sorry, but you'll have to go on so you won't be late. If Percival comes in this morning, I'll put him in another class for the rest of the day."

After a brief pep talk to the kids, Mrs. Foster stepped off the bus, and the driver started pulling out of the driveway. I sat down in one of the front seats, heavy of heart and without a speck of enthusiasm for the trip.

As the bus rounded the corner and headed out of the school driveway, one of the children shouted, "That sure is a fancy black motorcycle following us! That thing's purty!"

I looked back behind the bus and shouted to the top of my lungs!

"Stop! Stop the bus!"

The driver slammed on brakes, nearly causing the bus following him to crash into the back of us. Just as the bus came to a complete stop, the driver of the motorcycle pulled up beside the bus door, revving the engine and shouting something that none of us could discern.

The bus driver opened the door and just stared! There on the motorcycle sat a woman with long, curly, red hair that hung down to her waist. She was covered in shiny, black leather from her neck to her boots. Everything about her was black leather except for her head. It was totally uncovered, no sign of a helmet, and red, kinky hair flying everywhere!

Perched behind the lady in leather was Percival! He waved jauntily to me as I stared, open-mouthed at the spectacle in the doorway.

"Hey, Techr! Glad ya' didn't leave me. I overslept and missed the bus this mornin', so Ma brought me to school."

Percival hopped off the motorcycle and skipped up the steps of the bus.

"Can I sit with you, Techr? I can tell you all about the circus on the way, 'cause I've done seen it two times on TV. That be all right wid ya', Techr?" I finally breathed and hugged Percival to me.

"Sure, Big Guy, I'd be honored to have you sit with me. Actually, I was saving this seat just for you."

Percival smiled that lopsided smile of his and nudged me in the shoulder.

"Did'ya' see my Ma's motorcycle? Ain't it a beaut, Techr?"

"Yes…yes, it is a beauty all right. You ride it very much, Percival?"

"Naw…Ma won't let me less it's someum' special… like today when I missed the bus. But she rides it all the time to work and back and stuff."

"Does your Mama ever wear a helmet, Percival?"

"Well…she has one but she don't wear it much 'cause she said it messes up her hair."

I looked down at Percival's red, kinky hair, exactly like his mom's and said a silent prayer that he had arrived at school safe and sound. Boy, I loved that little kid…every irritating inch of him. We settled back on the seat of the bus and spent the rest of the trip talking about the circus.

THIRTY-ONE

THE SMELL OF COTTON CANDY, popcorn, and elephants filled my nostrils when we entered the huge coliseum. I had divided my twenty-two students into four groups so that each chaperone with my class had only five children to watch. I kept seven with me.

My heart fluttered with excitement as we scrambled to our seats in the top balcony. Anastasia managed to seat her children right next to mine, and my heart beat a little faster when she took the seat beside me. I was about as excited as all of my twenty-two students. Maybe more so.

Just as the music made a loud crescendo with an ear-splitting drum roll, and the ringmaster came to center stage, I felt a tug on my arm. I looked around to see Madalyn standing next to me.

"What's wrong, Madalyn? You need to be in your seat. The circus is about to begin!"

"I gotta go to the baffroom, Techr."

"Now! You can't hold it a little bit 'til we see the

beginning of the circus?"

Madalyn shook her head and her big baby blues took on a pleading look.

"I gotta go now!"

Reluctantly, I got up from my seat and took Madalyn by the hand. We stumbled across sets of feet all across the aisle and headed for the restroom down the large, circular hallway.

"Now you go do what you've got to do and come straight out, you hear?"

Madalyn hurried into the ladies restroom nodding her head as she went. After a few minutes she came out smiling, and we headed back to our seats.

Easing my long frame down into the seat next to Anastasia, I stared, excitedly, at the three rings of pomp and pageantry in progress on the circus floor. Just as I focused on the acrobatic act in the first ring, someone started tapping me on the shoulder. It was Josh.

I cupped my hands up to the blonde tykes' ears so that he could hear me over the noise.

"What do you want, Josh?"

"I gotta go to the baffroom, Techr, real bad!" Josh screwed up his little face like he was in great pain.

"Josh! Didn't you see me just take Madalyn to the restroom? Why didn't you go then?"

"I didn't haffa go then, Techr…but I do now, real bad!"

Rolling my eyes back in my head, I got up and grabbed Josh's hand. We stumbled over pairs of feet all the way down the aisle and headed for the men's restroom at the other end of the circular hallway. I waited impatiently outside the entrance until a smiling Josh reappeared a few minutes later.

I reached out and took Josh's hand in mine and led him back to our seats. By the time we got settled, the acrobatic stunts were over, and the ringmaster was announcing the next act. Jugglers! I just loved jugglers! Turning to Anastasia, I started to tell her how much I liked jugglers when I heard someone calling my name. I looked all around at my group of children when I saw a hand flailing in the air. It was Porsha.

I got up from my seat and went over to see what Porsha wanted.

Porsha whispered in my ear, "I gotta go, Techr."

I leaned back a bit and looked Porsha right in the eyes.

"Porsha, you can't go. We just got here, and the circus has a long way to go. Just sit back and enjoy it."

Porsha shook her head back and forth.

"No, Techr. I mean…I gotta go to the baffroom."

I couldn't believe my ears! Not another restroom trip!

"Porsha! Didn't you see me take Madalyn and Josh to the restroom just a few minutes ago? Why didn't you go then?"

Porsha hung her head.

"I didn't haff to go then, but I do now!"

Sighing deeply, I took Porsha's hand and led her over all the feet to take her to the restroom down the circular hall. When she came out a few minutes later, we trudged back to our seats. Porsha was smiling, but I had a scowl on my face. The juggling acts were over, and the ringmaster was center stage again announcing some dog tricks that would be in all three rings. So, I settled down in my seat to watch the dogs. Dogs were good…not as good as jugglers…but good.

But I'll never know how good the dog acts were because just as they came out, Mike, Raymond, and Randy scrambled over to where I was sitting. Of course, they all just had to go to the restroom. Mechanically, I got up from my seat and led the three boys back around the circular hallway to the restroom at the other end. I don't know what they did in there so long, but I suspect that restroom witnessed a contest of sorts from the three boys. Judging from the comments made when the boys returned, I'd venture to guess that Raymond was the winner! He was the only one of the three who wasn't splattered with wet drops all over him!

When the boys and I returned to our seats, the wild animals were being led to the rings by their trainers. I just caught a glimpse of the King of the Jungle before Bonni and Beth began to tug at my sleeve. Clinching my mouth together, I all but hissed at the girls.

"What? Don't tell me! You have to go to the restroom! Am I right?"

Without even giving the girls a chance to answer, I jumped up from my seat and grabbed both of their hands. Away we headed to the restroom. I didn't even have to look at the signs anymore. I knew the way by heart!

It seemed like an eternity before Bonni and Beth came

out of the restroom. They were giggling hysterically.

"What is so funny, girls?" I asked, disgustedly. The girls giggled even harder, both trying to talk through their fits of laughing.

"Hee...hee...hee...ugh...Techr...this real fat ...lady...hee...hee...got stuck in one...of the bathroom stalls...hee...hee...and she can't get out...hee...hee...and she looks so funny...hee...hee...stuck in that door...hee...hee."

I stared at Beth in disbelief!

"Beth, is she still stuck in the door?"

Beth and Bonni looked at each other again and laughed even harder. I knelt down and put my hands on the girls' shoulders.

"Bonni! Beth! Answer me! Is the lady still stuck in the door?"

Still laughing, both girls nodded their heads in the affirmative. It was then that I heard the lady in the restroom yelling. I looked around for someone to help the poor lady, but everyone seemed to be in the arena, watching the circus. Everyone except for two little girls, one fat lady stuck in a restroom stall, and me!

As the stuck lady's screams got louder, I knew I had to do something. Grabbing Beth and Bonni's hands, I headed into the lady's restroom, sweating profusely as I went. Praying, too!

What greeted me was a sight to behold! A very big lady, perhaps the FAT LADY from the circus, was indeed jammed between the potty and the door of the stall. The door only swung backwards, so there was no way to get the lady out with the door in the way.

"Stand back, girls," I told Bonni and Beth. "Stand over against the wall on the other side. I've got to take this door off, and I don't want it to fall on you."

Then I looked at the poor, embarrassed lady stuck in the door.

"Don't worry, Miss. I'll have you out of there in a minute."

I reached in my pocket and pulled out my old, trusty scout knife that 'Techr' had given me for my tenth birthday. Carefully I removed the hinges from the door, expecting the door to fall towards me at any minute. But it didn't. I stooped down and grabbed the door from the bottom and pulled with all my might. I heard the lady behind the door whimpering like a small kitten, when all of a sudden the door dislodged from her massive body. I went sailing across the restroom floor with the door of the restroom stall held tightly in my hands.

I don't remember seeing the fat lady leave the stall, and if she thanked me at all, I didn't hear her. I guess she was too embarrassed over the whole situation, so she just left the restroom quickly.

As I was getting off the floor of the lady's restroom and setting the door of the stall over to one side, an older lady came in. After giving me an odd look she left, shaking her head and mumbling under her breath, something about all the weirdoes in the world. I took Bonni and Beth's hands, and we headed back to our seats.

Climbing over all the children to get to my unused seat, I looked over my class to see if anyone else needed to make a trip to the restroom before I sat down. Every face was focused on the elephants that were standing on their back legs, walking around the ring. Quietly, I made my way back to my seat.

No sooner had I settled into my seat than I heard my name being called…again. I didn't even have to look around to see who was calling me. I dropped my head in despair.

"Tethu! Tethu! I dotta doe to da baffoom."

Marcus Jones. Well, at least I could understand him now.

Once again, I crawled over the children and stood in the aisle. Putting my hands on my hips, I leered at my group.

"Boys and Girls," I said much too loudly. "If you need to go to the restroom, come now or you will not go until the circus is over! Is that clear?"

Iouli and Percival jumped up and followed Marcus over to where I was standing. We made a quick trip to the restroom, and hurried back to our seats to catch the elephants before they were led away. But we were too late. A small car full of clowns was riding around the circus stage while the coliseum crew began to set up for the flying trapeze acts.

I looked over my group with contempt and anger. They were laughing wildly at the clowns as the funny looking creatures piled from the tiny little car. My heart melted when I saw the excitement and joy on each face. So, I had missed all of the circus up to this point. But at least I would get to see the trapeze acts…and the grand finale parade.

I stepped over all of the feet once again and found my seat beside Anastasia. She looked over and patted my hand.

"I'm sorry you've had to take so many of your students to the restroom and miss most of the circus. I can't believe my students didn't ask to go. You haven't had a very good time, have you?"

I didn't even grace her comments with an answer. I had missed the opening parade, the jugglers, all of the animals, including the elephants, and even the dog tricks. I didn't get to see the tall man, but I did see the FAT LADY…up close and personal. I smiled at the cute first grade teacher beside me.

"Believe me…I got to see more than you realize."

It probably was a good thing that I went to the rescue of the fat lady in the restroom, because as it turned out, I did not get to see the trapeze acts nor the final parade. Jessica and Mary Anne had to make emergency trips to the "world famous restroom" during the last few minutes of the circus performances, even after my threats that no one else would go. Actually, Mary Anne didn't even make it. She wet her pants right outside the restroom door. I was probably cleaning up the puddle when the grand parade was marching around the arena for the last time. When the girls and I headed back to our seats, everyone was filing out to go to the buses. Anastasia had my class walking beside hers, all of the children talking at once about what a wonderful circus it had been.

I'll never know if the circus was good or not. I do know that I can locate the ladies' and men's restrooms in the upper deck of the coliseum in record time; that chaperones on a field trip are virtually useless; and the fat lady needs to leave the door open when she goes in a restroom stall.

THIRTY-TWO

IT WAS PRETTY OBVIOUS THAT I was a little bit peeved with my students as we rode the bus back to the school that afternoon. I didn't say too much, just sat quietly in my seat at the front of the bus and listened to the chatter of the excited children as they recalled the events of the day.

I breathed deeply and pretended to be asleep when I heard Bonni tell somebody about 'Mr. Techr' going into the girls' restroom and taking a door down to see a lady who was in there. I sure hoped that story didn't get all blown out of proportion. That's all I needed after the reputation I'd already established!

When we finally arrived back at the school, all of the parents were waiting for their children except for Percival's mother. After standing around with Percival for nearly an hour, and repeated phone calls to his home, I put my arm around the little fellow's shoulders and told him I'd take him home.

"Ya' mean I git to ride in ya' car, Techr? That'll be fun!"

I looked down at the excitement on Percival's face.

"I don't really have a cool car, Percival. I'm still driving your other teacher's old rusty car."

Percival turned his freckled nose up to me and smiled.

"Tha's all right, Techr, long as I git ta' ride side'ja."

The tense moments of the day somehow faded as Percival and I rode along together to his house. He jabbered nonstop about the tigers and how he could have 'whupped 'em' into shape. To hear Percival tell it, he could have run that circus single-handedly, and I couldn't help but smile at the little fellow's boastful attitude.

I followed Percival's directions until we made the last turn onto a dirt street that led to a rundown trailer park. It didn't take a Philadelphia lawyer to spot which trailer was Percival's. A shiny black motorcycle, gleaming in the fading rays of the sun, was parked in front of a small, dilapidated trailer at the end of the street.

Pointing to the trailer, I asked, "Percival, is that where you live?"

Percival looked down at his shoes and shook his head.

"Yeah, that's it. Looks like Mama is home. Wonda why she didn't answer the phone?"

I hunched my shoulders and wondered the same thing as Percival and I got out of the car and walked over the weed-infested yard to the trailer. Just as I started to knock, the door opened. Percival's mom stood there, still dressed in her black leather.

"Oh, it's just you, Perce. I thought it was Slick coming to pick me up."

"You going out agin tonight, Ma?"

"Okay, Perce, don't start! You know I go out every Friday night with Slick. Come on in the house now and find you something to do. Aunt Linda'll be here t'reckly to watch you."

Turning to me, the lady in leather, alias Percival's mom, glared with a look of icy indifference.

"Who're you? Perce's teacher?"

I nodded.

"We waited for you at the school for nearly an hour, Ma'am, and we called, too, but no one answered. So on my way home, I decided to drop Percival by your house."

"Well, you better get on down the road now, 'cause Slick don't like no men hanging around here." No thank you, no explanation, or anything!

I turned and walked back to the car, feeling for the world that I should not have taken Percival home. I looked back at the trailer when I drove out of the rutted driveway and couldn't help but smile when I saw Percival standing at the window, saluting me of all things. I saluted back and drove home to begin a much needed weekend.

THIRTY-THREE

IT WAS A LITTLE PAST SIX in the evening when I arrived home. The thoughts of the day swirled through my brain as I popped a TV dinner in the microwave. I checked the answering machine where I found twelve messages from my dad. I listened to a couple of them only to discern that he had found out somehow that I was not at the university. I deleted the rest of Dad's recordings, not really in the mood to hear his displeasure of my recent decision making.

Dad had an uncanny way of keeping up with my schedule. It was almost time for my finals, and I'm sure he knew that. What he didn't know was that I had planned to devote the entire weekend to studying for them. I had to if I was even going to come close to passing a single course!

All weekend I studied. I studied when I ate. I studied when I walked. I studied when I went to the bathroom. I even studied in my sleep. The phone rang a good many times, but I ignored it, afraid it would disturb my keen concentration.

By Monday morning my brain was so full of medical terms, formulas, and lists of symptomatic ailments that I could hardly think of anything else. I drove the old car to school, still reciting lists of memorized paraphernalia. I knew without a doubt that by Thursday, the day of my finals, I'd be ready.

Mrs. Foster was standing in the hallway when I entered the building.

"Good morning, Johnny. How was the circus?"

"Don't ask me, Mrs. Foster. I spent the day escorting children back and forth to the restroom. However, I did get to see the fat lady! I'll have to tell you about her sometime."

Mrs. Foster laughed. "I believe I've already heard that story this morning. Children do tell everything they know."

I swallowed hard at that news. All I needed was another rumor floating around the school. I hurried to explain.

"This real big lady got stuck in a stall in the restroom, and I took the door off the stall so she could get out. That's all!"

I watched the merriment dance in the principal's eyes as she laughed. "Johnny, you do somehow manage to get yourself in the worst predicaments. But I know you. The perfect gentleman…your daddy's son. You don't need to worry about the rumors. I'll put a stop to them."

"Thanks, Mrs. Foster. Oh, by the way, I need to be off on Thursday and Friday of this week. I have finals to take at the university."

"Sure, Johnny, I'll get you covered. But you will be back to finish out the year, won't you?"

"You bet, Mrs. Foster. How could I stay away? I have my second monthly check coming in next week, all $923.00, and you never know when I might be needed to rescue one of you girls from the stalls of death!"

I could hear the principal's laughter all the way down the hall as I made my way to my classroom. When I opened the door, the smells of floor cleaner and children's sweat hit me in the face. Throwing my jacket over the back of 'Techr's' chair, my chair now, I walked quickly back to the doorway, crossed my arms, and leaned against the doorjamb. It was time for the first bus to arrive.

Pretty soon I heard little feet stomping and scuffling down the hallway. I strained my eyes until I recognized the same faces that had kept me from seeing the circus, and my chest expanded a notch or two. Lawdy! How I loved these annoying, small-bladdered, smelly little kids!

THIRTY-FOUR

THE THREE DAYS BEFORE I had to leave to go take my finals were uneventful for the most part. Not counting Brennan socking Luke in the nose for taking his ball at recess and Cameron stealing Tremaine's homework, erasing the name and putting his name in its place, the week went okay.

I left school early on Wednesday to catch my flight to Atlanta. Anastasia took me to the airport and lingered around until I had to go through the security check. An unexpected chill passed over me when I turned to wave goodbye to my little teacher friend. I shook it off and walked quickly to wait for my flight.

I arrived in Atlanta late that night and rented a car to drive the rest of the way to the university. I really wanted to call Mom and Dad, but my better judgment took over when I thought of all the lectures I'd receive from my parents.

The guys were all still up, cramming as usual, when I

arrived at the old green house. Most of them seemed genuinely glad to see me, slapping me on the back and catching me up on the latest escapades on campus. It was nearly three in the morning when I finally went to sleep.

My first exam on Thursday morning was a breeze. The second was pretty easy, too. But when I got to the last one for that day, either my fatigue or lack of attending classes the entire semester got the better of me. I just didn't know anything that was on the exam. Nothing!

By five o'clock that afternoon I was either brain-washed or brain-dead, one or the other. I fell into my bed and went sound asleep only to awaken to Lynn poking me in the arm.

"Hey, wake up, Johnny. Some fine sounding woman is on the phone asking for you."

Thinking it must be Anastasia on the line, I stumbled to the phone.

"Hello?"

"Johnny? I can't believe I'm finally talking to you after all these months. How is my favorite baby brother doing?"

"Tara? Hey, Sis. How'd you find me?"

"I have my ways, Johnny. You know I'm a regular bloodhound! So, how have you been doing? I hear from Dad that you're still at 'Techr's' house. I've tried to call you there, but you don't ever answer the phone. What's going on?"

"Tara, I have so much to tell you. Are you sitting down? Tara, I'm teaching! I took over 'Techr's' class after she died. Sis, did you hear me? I'm teaching, and I love it!"

There were a few moments of silence before Tara

responded.

"I already know you've been filling in for 'Techr'. Believe me, Dad rants and raves about it all the time. But, Johnny, we all thought you'd give that up when a good replacement could be found. Why are you still there?"

I cleared my throat, searching for the right words to use.

"Tara, I hadn't planned on staying this long. But, those kids lost their teacher, and when I came in to take over for a few days, they got attached to me…and I got attached to them, too. They need me, Sis. I wish you could come and see them. There's Mary Anne who nobody messes with, and little Madalyn, who has the biggest blue eyes you've ever seen, and beautiful Jessica who already knows how to flirt with the boys, and Josh and Brennan, and Iouli, my little Russian boy, and I know I'm not supposed to have favorites, but Tara, you just have to meet Percival! I just love that bossy, freckled-faced, red-headed kid!"

"Whoa, Little Brother! I get the picture! You're hooked on this teacher thing, aren't you?"

"I'm afraid I am, Tara! Everyday is an adventure. I never know what's going to happen from one day to the next. I know all the reasons I shouldn't be doing this, the main one being the pitiful pay teachers get. But, Tara, I'm sorry! I love it!"

"What about Dad's dreams for you to follow in his footsteps, Johnny? He's going to be crushed!"

"I know, Sis. You mentioned that I don't answer the phone. That's why. I can't talk to Dad right now. Can you talk to him for me, Tara? He dotes on you. You're the perfect daughter who always does the right things. Please, Sis! Talk to him for me!"

"I'll try, Johnny. But he's got to hear it from you. But I'll try."

"Thanks, Tara. You're the best! So…is anything new going on with you?"

There was a slight pause on the other end of the line.

"As a matter of fact, there is, Johnny. Speaking of teachers, I've been dating a teacher for the last few months, and it's getting kind of serious! How would you like to be in a wedding this summer?"

"What? You're getting married? To a teacher? I love it! When do I get to meet this wonderful fellow?"

Tara laughed. "Soon, Johnny, soon. Dr. Lanford said I can take several days off in a few weeks to get my wedding planned. Maybe 'My Teacher,' and I can fly out to see you for a day or two. How does that sound? I know you and Scott will have a lot in common. I've got to run now, Johnny. Take care and call me sometime. I'll let you know how the conversation with Dad goes, and hope to see you soon!"

"Bye, Sis. I love you!" I hung up the phone and tried to hit the books again. It was hard to concentrate after the conversation with my only sibling, the sister who had told on me and stuck up for me more times in my life than I could count. So I more or less held the notes for the exams the next day, pretending to use my time wisely.

After my last two finals that were surprisingly easy, I broke it to the guys abruptly that I was taking my car back to South Carolina. They all but cried when I piled the BMW full of my stuff and drove away. But it was something I had to do. I knew I probably wouldn't be back, and I needed to bring closure to this chapter in my life.

It took me about six hours to get back to 'Techr's' house. I felt like a dog for not going by to see my parents, but I knew that was something I couldn't do right then. I promised myself I'd make it up to them later and prayed to God that they would come around to my way of thinking.

But they didn't. At least, Dad didn't understand. Tara called the next day and said she'd tried to make Dad understand what I was doing, but said Dad was furious. So I prayed again, this time for God to keep Dad so busy that he didn't have time to think about me. Then I spent the rest of Sunday afternoon planning my lessons for the coming week.

THIRTY-FIVE

MONDAY MORNING loomed bright and warm as the new month of May made its appearance, and with it, only three weeks left in the school year. I worked frantically with my students, especially on reading and math, so they would be prepared for the second grade. I felt really good about all but two of them, so I worked it out with their parents for me to help them after school each day.

All of the children got antsy as the year drew to a close, and I found I had to constantly think of new ways to keep their attention. Being a big Atlanta Braves fan myself, I gave all the students a Braves' baseball player name, and I even blew one of my checks on baseball hats for each one of them. We spent a lot of time every day learning new words and facts by rounding the bases as Major League baseball players. The kids loved it. Iouli said he'd rather be a Yankee, but he hit a lot of home runs under the name of Chipper. The amazing thing was that the children were actually learning while they were having fun.

A week went by…then two. The Friday before the last week of school, I stayed rather late after school, carefully planning the last week's activities. I wanted every child in my classroom to remember his or her first grade class as something really special. When I was satisfied I had it all planned, I packed my denim bag with scissors, glue, a stapler, magic markers, and construction paper…all the good things teachers just have to take around with them…and headed for home. I was so lost in my thoughts and plans for the next week that I didn't notice the maroon Explorer parked in my driveway until I pulled up behind it.

My heart sank! Dad! There was no way I could escape! With great dread and trepidation I opened the door and walked into 'Techr's' house. There he sat. Looking. His arms folded across his chest…just looking.

"Hi, Dad," I said in a voice about two octaves higher than mine usually was. "How're you doing?"

Dr. Johnathon Adams, the renowned heart surgeon who had surpassed all odds by overcoming a childhood of abuse and neglect, my Dad, continued to stare at me with those piercing brown eyes of his.

"I think a more fitting question might be, 'How are you doing,' Johnny?" Not a smile, not a blink of an eye. I felt like a six year old with my hand caught in the cookie jar.

"Well, I'm doing just fine, Dad. Just fine. And you?"

I got 'The Look' that had brought me down to size so many times when I was growing up.

"I'm not doing too well, Johnny. You see, I have one son…that would be you…who was a straight 'A' student in his second year at medical school. And this only son…you… the pride and joy of my heart, has for some idiotic reason decided to chunk his entire career for a fill-in teacher's job that will surely amount to nothing. To put it bluntly, Johnny, I am confused, angry, and mad as the devil at you! What's come over you, Johnny? Tara told me that you took your finals after neglecting to attend a single class the entire semester. And…now…you're back here! So… what's with that, Johnny? Can you please explain to me what in the world you think you're doing?"

I sank down in the old comfortable chair facing Dad and put my head in my hands. After a rather long period of silence, I finally found my voice.

"Dad, I know you don't understand. Sometimes I don't understand why I'm still here either. I had good intentions to stay only long enough to get 'Techr's' things in order. But then, the principal called me and asked me to take over 'Techr's' class for a few days until she could find a replacement. And out of love and respect for 'Techr', I tried to help out…just for a few days."

"But, Dad, Mrs. Foster couldn't find anyone in the dead of winter who was qualified to teach, and those little kids needed someone. So I stayed a little longer…and then a little longer…and before I knew it, I just couldn't leave."

Dad frowned and shook his head. "Johnny, you are certainly NOT qualified to teach first graders or any grade for that matter! What do you know about teaching?"

"You're right, Dad. I'm not qualified. But I'm learning, everyday. And I care, Dad. A substitute off the street doesn't care about those kids. No…I take that back. A few of them do care. But most of them just come and get through each day, give loads of busy work, and wait for their checks to come in the mail. But not me, Dad! I really care! What would little Robin have done when her sorry excuse for a dad shaved her head bald if I hadn't been there for her? And what about Percival? Who would have taken him home after the trip to the circus if a substitute had been in charge instead of me? And then there's Marcus, who can't speak plainly…and…and Iouli, the little boy from Russia…and…and…"

"Stop right there, Johnny! You can't be the savior of the world! Listen to me, Johnny! Anybody can be a teacher! Anybody! Not everyone has the tenacity nor the brains to be a doctor! You were born to be a doctor, Johnny! A great doctor who will save the lives of many more children and adults than any teacher ever will!"

"Dad! I can't believe I'm hearing what you're saying! Just where do you think you would be if it weren't for a teacher who saved your life?"

Dad looked down at the floor with a look of melancholy on his usually strong face.

"That's different, Johnny. 'Techr' was in a class all by herself! There'll never be another like her."

"So you're saying I can never measure up to 'Techr,' is that it? Don't you think I know that, Dad? 'Techr' was special; probably to every kid who ever walked into her classroom. She made a difference…she changed lives…just look at you, Dad. You've said over and over that you are what you are today because one first grade teacher cared enough to make a difference in your life!"

"I want to make a difference in children's lives, too, Dad. I know I can't be 'Techr,' but I can be a teacher who cares and has compassion and loves children."

"Why can't you do that as a doctor, Johnny? Think of all the thousands of lives you could touch as a doctor! Think, Johnny! You're still caught up in the emotion of 'Techr's' death, but you've got to let that go and get on with your life! I can't let you throw away all you've worked for to try to carry on 'Techr's' legacy! I just won't let you do it!"

Just as I was losing the battle with my dad, the phone rang. Without a spark of spirit, I answered it on the third ring. I came to attention when I heard the principal's voice on the other end of the line.

"Oh, Johnny, I'm so glad I caught you! There's been an accident, Johnny! It's Percival's mother. The hospital called me because they can't locate her sister who lives in Augusta. Percival's here. His mother's boyfriend brought him over, and he's beside himself! Can you come over to the hospital? And hurry, Johnny! Percival needs you!"

With a sick feeling in the pit of my stomach, I hung up the phone and rushed to grab my keys from the corner table where I had dropped them earlier.

Dad followed me, looking every bit as bewildered and confused as I felt.

"What happened, Johnny? What's wrong?"

Somewhat in a daze, I answered. "That was the

principal. She said there has been an accident, and that Percival needs me." Looking Heavenward, I cried, "Not Percival, Dear Lord! This can't be happening! Not to my freckled-faced, red-headed Percival!"

I rushed out the door with my dad close on my heels.

"I'll go with you, Son. Maybe I can help. I'll drive. Tell me where to go."

Dad and I jumped in his Explorer and literally flew down the street toward the hospital. Inside the car was total silence except for the hum of the engine and my repeated prayers for God to look after Percival. That was one of the longest trips of my life!

THIRTY-SIX

AFTER PARKING ILLEGALLY, Dad and I rushed into the emergency room at the end of the hospital. Looking frantically around, I spotted Mrs. Foster stooping near the patient entrance of the examining rooms. I walked over to the principal with Dad close on my heels. That's when I saw Percival. He was crouched in a tight ball, leaning into the doorframe, his head resting on the top of his scrawny little knees.

I knelt down next to him and gently put my hand on his shoulder. He quickly jerked away. I looked back at Dad who hunched his shoulders and said nothing. Turning back to my red-headed little friend, I spoke as softly as I could.

"Percival, it's me…Techr." I put my hand once again on Percival's shoulder. "Hey, Little Buddy. You okay?"

Very slowly Percival looked up at me. His blue eyes were swollen from crying, and his freckled face was splotched with tear stains and grime. In a quivery voice, very much unlike the take-charge child that I knew,

Percival started talking.

"Hey, Techr. I knew you'd come. I jest knew you would. Ma got hurt real bad, Techr. She had a wreck on her motorcycle coming home from work today, and she's hurt real bad. They won't let me go see her. Why won't they let me go see her, Techr? I can probably make her feel better. Slick said she hurt her head, and I always rub her head when it hurts and make it feel all better."

Percival grabbed both of my sleeves in a death grip. "Please, Techr! Tell'em to let me go see my mama so I can make her feel all better!" The tears started to flow again as Percival clutched my sleeves and looked straight into my face.

I glanced over at Mrs. Foster, and she shook her head.

"Percival, you'll probably get to see your mother in a little while. In the meantime, I want you to meet somebody." I stood up, bringing Percival to his feet as I stood. Placing my arm firmly around his shoulders, I maneuvered the sad little fellow to where my dad was standing behind me.

"Percival, I want you to meet my dad. He used to go to the school where you go now. Actually, he was in the same first grade classroom as you are now. He may have even used the same desk. He's a doctor now."

Percival perked up a little when he met my dad.

"You shore 'nuff went to my school? That musta been a hundret years ago, you so old." Dad and I both chuckled but stopped abruptly when we saw the sadness creep back on Percival. He turned his teary eyes up to me.

"Techr, ya' lucky to haf' a daddy. I ain't got one. It's jest my mama and me…and sometimes my Aunt Linda stays wif' us….'specially if she's on the outs wif' Unca' Robert."

I looked over at Dad and smiled. He didn't smile back, but had a look of wonder and amazement on his face. Pulling my eyes away from Dad's staring look, I once again knelt down to Percival and put my hands on his shoulders.

Percival focused his tear-filled eyes on mine.

"Techr, my mama's gonna be all right, ain't she? She's gotta be all right 'cause I ain't got nobody else!"

I hugged Percival to me, and he sobbed loudly, with occasional swipes of his snotty nose on my shirt. My own tears mixed with his as I mourned…not for the mother who was fighting for her very life…but for the child who needed a mother, black leather and all.

Percival clung to me for the better part of the night; sometimes holding my hand; sometimes crouched into my strong embrace; and sometimes nestled on my lap, dozing fitfully in his tortured sleep.

About four o'clock the next morning, the doctor on call came out to tell us that Percival's mama didn't make it. She had died from multiple head injuries sustained from the motorcycle accident. She had not been wearing a helmet.

Percival's Aunt Linda had arrived by then. She took the sobbing boy from my lap and left the hospital. As I sadly watched Percival walk through the revolving doors, I broke down and cried like a baby for the little freckled-faced boy who would never see his mama again.

After a few moments, I felt the strong hand of my dad touch my shoulder.

"Come on, Son. Let's go home. You need to get a little rest, because that boy's going to need his teacher tomorrow."

THIRTY-SEVEN

SUNDAY WAS A SUNNY, WARM DAY filled with a gentle breeze, birds singing, and bright, yellow jonquils in full bloom all along the roadside. I marveled at the beautiful signs of life as Dad and I rode in silence to the cemetery. It was the first time either one of us had been back to where 'Techr' had been laid to rest just four short months earlier.

Dad parked the car on the circular drive that surrounded the gravesites, and we walked quietly up the hill to join the handful of mourners who had come to pay their last respects to Percival's mom. I nodded to Mrs. Foster and Anastasia as I walked up to stand near the edge of the small gathering. Dad walked up beside me and looked down, his hands clasped tightly behind his back.

One lone, shiny black car pulled up close to the canvas tarp that flapped in the wind over the mound of fresh dirt, hidden for the moment under a piece of green, outdoor carpet. The car idled for a minute or two before the engine was silenced, and the driver came around to open the back passenger door.

Two people emerged from the car. The first was the sister of the deceased, Aunt Linda. Sliding out behind her was Percival. I couldn't help but stare at my little student, dressed in a new, blue suit, shiny black shoes, and hair slicked down so that no sign of kinky red curls stuck out anywhere.

Percival walked with his head down, and he held tightly to his aunt's hand as they made their way to the first row of seats under the open tent. The minister from the Methodist Church had just begun to read the usual verses of scripture about "walking in the valley of the shadow of death and fearing no evil" when Percival looked up. His eyes locked in on mine immediately, and through his tears, I saw a faint glimmer of a crooked smile. I smiled back and waved, my heart breaking into a thousand pieces for this sad, very brave little boy.

The service was short, and Percival was herded out to the waiting car by his aunt as soon as the minister said the final amen. The other people scattered quickly, leaving Dad and me standing alone at the gravesite. I stared at the grave as the funeral attendants began filling in the hole with the fresh dirt from under the green carpet.

There was only one bouquet of flowers…the ones I had sent. There were no rose petals or notes or remembrances of any kind left at the grave. There was nothing to honor this mother who had lived a short life and left behind only one, very small, red-headed, strong-willed boy as her legacy. I looked at her fresh grave and cried for this young mother who would never know the wonderful son she had given to the world.

After a prayer of my own, I turned to my dad who was standing beside me.

"Dad, I'm going to walk up the hill and see 'Techr' for a minute. You want to come along?"

Dad nodded his head, draped his strong arm around my shoulders, and we headed up the steep hill to see 'Techr.' After taking only a few steps, Dad stopped walking and turned to face me.

"Johnny, I was wrong about you. You do know how to be a teacher. I have been so proud of you over the last two days. You have really been good with Percival. Do you know who you've reminded me of during all of this? 'Techr!' Johnny, you're just like her!"

"Oh, don't get me wrong! I still think you'd make a fine doctor, too. But, the great doctors come from the great teachers. You were right, Son. Where would I be today if it hadn't been for a teacher who changed the course of my life forever? Go on, Son! Become that teacher you so desperately want to be! You have my blessing!"

Dad looked up the hill and pointed to the spot where 'Techr' was buried.

"And I know there will be one special Angel in Heaven smiling down on you and cheering you on each day of your life." Dad brushed away a tear, put his arm back around my shoulders, and we continued walking up the lonely hill together.

When we reached 'Techr's' grave, we just stood there, my dad and me, crying silently. All kinds of fond memories flooded my brain when suddenly I felt a warm little hand reach for my own.

I glanced down, and there stood Percival, looking up at me, his freckled, small hand clasped tightly to mine. He looked so tiny and so alone.

"Hey, Techr. I jest come to tell ya' good-bye. I gotta go live with Aunt Linda in 'Gusta, and we fixin' to leave. Techr, they never did let me see Ma. I might coulda' made her head feel better, but they wouldn't let me see her. But I 'member how she looked, don't you?"

I nodded to Percival as I knelt down on one knee.

"Yeah, I remember. Your Mama was a real pretty lady, with hair just like yours." I reached out and touched a red curl that had managed to escape all the gel that was holding it down.

Percival shook his head up and down as his eyes filled with tears.

"Well, I gotta go now, Techr. Aunt Linda tole me to hurry back so we can git on the road. She wants to get to "Gusta 'fore dark."

I stared at this precious child, trying to memorize every detail about him. His teary, little eyes stared right back into mine, and before I could stop myself, I gathered Percival tightly in my arms and just about squeezed the breath out of him.

Finally releasing him, I said softly, "Go on, Percival. Aunt Linda's waiting. She's a real nice lady, your Aunt

Linda. You'll be all right. But remember…if you ever need me, I'll be right here. Okay?"

"Okay, Techr." Percival started walking down the hill when he turned suddenly and yelled back at me.

"Techr! Ya' know something? For a Techr who ain't no real Techr, ya' ain't haff bad!"